Candle in a Bottle

Conversation Pieces

A Small Paperback Series from Aqueduct Press
Subscriptions available: www.aqueductpress.com

About the Aqueduct Press Conversation Pieces Series

The feminist engaged with sf is passionately interested in challenging the way things are, passionately determined to understand how everything works. It is my constant sense of our feminist-sf present as a grand conversation that enables me to trace its existence into the past and from there see its trajectory extending into our future. A genealogy for feminist sf would not constitute a chart depicting direct lineages but would offer us an ever-shifting, fluid mosaic, the individual tiles of which we will probably only ever partially access. What could be more in the spirit of feminist sf than to conceptualize a genealogy that explicitly manifests our own communities across not only space but also time?

Aqueduct's small paperback series, Conversation Pieces, aims to both document and facilitate the "grand conversation." The Conversation Pieces series presents a wide variety of texts, including short fiction (which may not always be sf and may not necessarily even be feminist), essays, speeches, manifestoes, poetry, interviews, correspondence, and group discussions. Many of the texts are reprinted material, but some are new. The grand conversation reaches at least as far back as Mary Shelley and extends, in our speculations and visions, into the continually-created future. In Jonathan Goldberg's words, "To look forward to the history that will be, one must look at and retell the history that has been told." And that is what Conversation Pieces is all about.

L. Timmel Duchamp

Jonathan Goldberg, "The History That Will Be" in Louise Fradenburg and Carla Freccero, eds., *Premodern Sexualities* (New York and London: Routledge, 1996)

Published by Aqueduct Press
PO Box 95787
Seattle, WA 98145-2787
www.aqueductpress.com

ISBN: 0-11-000222-9
         978-0-11-000222-4

First published in slightly different version in
The Magazine of Fantasy and Science Fiction, Volume 91, October/
November, 1996

Cover Design by Lynne Jensen Lampe
Cover candle-lantern illustration by Kathryn Wilham
Book Design by Kathryn Wilham
Original Block Print of Mary Shelley by Justin Kempton:
www.writersmugs.com

Cover photo of Pleiades Star Cluster
NASA Hubble Telescope Images, STScI-2004-20
http://hubble.nasa.gov/image-gallery/astronomy-images.html
Credit: NASA, ESA, and AURA/Caltech

Printed in the USA

Conversation Pieces
Volume 13

Candle in a Bottle

A Novella

by

Carolyn Ives Gilman

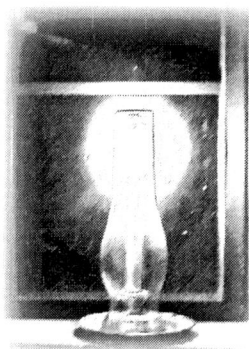

Chapter 1

The storm hit just as the two travelers were coming to the summit of L'Arc du Sol Pass. All morning the sun had been bright at their backs as they had climbed through pine-covered slopes. When the trail rose above the tree line, they should have been able to see the whole Vaudry Range spread before them, the granite palisades of Mont Chatoyer to the west. Instead, there was only a blinding wall of snow, a visible white noise driven by a reckless wind.

Dominique trudged along in the path Gabriel was breaking. Ahead, his brother was only a snow-caked capote with a nylon pack and shaggy sheepskin boots grown enormous with iceballs. He called ahead, "Hey, Gabe, is this what you meant by 'It'll be fun'?"

Gabriel looked back with a tense frown. His dark hair was plastered down with wet, and the mesh skullcap of his headnet glistened with drops. He said, "Keep your mind on the trail, Nika."

It had been Gabriel's idea to cut across the mountains on foot instead of taking the sane way around by road. It would have taken at least a week, and more money than Gabriel wanted to spend, to go by public transport. He had argued, "It's only three days to the Institut Sorel by foot, if we cut across the pass. Come on, Nika, you're

1

the experiential one; it's your chance to have a real flesh adventure. It'll be fun."

At the time Dominique had rolled his eyes, knowing what kind of fun you could get into on mountain trails so close to winter. But a glance from their mother had told him he had to go. It didn't matter that he was the younger brother; he had always been the one who had to watch out for Gabriel. And Gabriel was in such a mood that he would risk his life hazarding the pass alone rather than give up.

Gabriel had had all summer to make up his mind to go, but he had frittered away the months, indecision alternating with bitter dissatisfaction. He was the nethead in the family, smart and ambitious to do more than work in his mother's shop. But the lack of any obvious alternative had kept him at home, wasting the days in political tele-caucuses with others as malcontent as he, his irritation growing till his family had all begged him to do something, anything. Finally, when it was already too late in the season, so that failure was almost inevitable, he had decided to consult the Oracle at the Institut Sorel.

The trail was going down now, writhing to and fro like a thing tormented. Dominique thought he could glimpse a shadow of trees ahead—a good sign. As they came to the last exposed switchback, Gabriel stopped in his tracks and began fiddling with the recorder under his coat. "I've got to change spools," he said.

Dominique stood and waited. Gabriel was recording this whole trek, though the resolution of his equipment would stink. At least a headnet couldn't record the cold or wet; that might improve things. But Dominique still couldn't imagine who would want to experience a mountain hike through Gabriel's eyes. He missed so much.

In the willful way of mountain weather, a shaft of sunlight lit the slope ahead. The view momentarily cleared.

Below them lay a circular valley with a single outcrop of rock rising at its center. Upon that lone spire were the buildings of the Institut, like natural outgrowths of the rock itself.

"Gabriel, look!" Dominique said.

"Just a second," Gabriel said, fumbling with the recorder.

"It's Sorel!" Dominique said.

The sunlight faded, leaving the scene gray and ominous. Gabriel finally looked up, his hair running in rivulets down his high forehead. "That's Sorel!" he said, as if his brother wouldn't know. Dominique realized he was speaking to the recorder. "You're looking at the center of the intellectual universe, Dominique. That's the place where the true spirit of Renaissance Dernier learning is kept alive."

The clouds closed in again. Dominique tried to shake some of the snow from his boots and pack. He felt like a walking glacier. "I hope they have hot baths."

Gabriel didn't dignify this with an answer. He headed down the trail again at a pace so fast Dominique nearly had to jog to keep up.

Dominique had never shared his brother's restless, searching nature. Because he was big, muscular, and easygoing, everyone had expected him to excel in sports or a physical profession. But all he had ever wanted to do was work in his mother's shop where the finest seismic monitors in the world were made, piecing together photonic components under the microscope with his blunt, dextrous fingers.

It was almost dark by the time they reached the valley and struck out across featureless farmland. Here, in open fields, the storm truly surrounded them. Right, left, above, and below blended into a limitless chaos of white—no boundaries, no differentiation to make sense of what they saw. Dominique trudged along, sure only of one direction, down.

They struck a road just outside the village of Sous-Sorel. Soon the glow of streetlights cut through the disordered night. As they slogged through knee-deep snow down the deserted main street, fantasies of dry clothes and a hot sauna filled Dominique's mind.

In better weather, the shops along the main street catered to the droves of pilgrims who flocked to consult the Oracle about their futures. Now the streetlights, veiled in haloes of snow, shone only on closed doors and curtained windows. Gabriel stopped, his eye caught by the single lit window on the street.

"Look, a bookstore," he said.

"Just what I wanted," Dominique groaned.

"They'll have free coffee. All bookstores do."

They entered along with a gust of snowy wind. There was no one in sight, so they dumped their packs by the door and went looking for the coffee, leaving white footprints on the carpet. When Dominique found the samovar, he poured two steaming cups. Gabriel was wrinkling his nose at the racks of pastel-covered sample books around them. "Inspirational garbage," he said. "You'd think that here…"

"Pilgrims?" said a sardonic voice. In the doorway to a back room stood a stooped man with thin, graying hair and an expression as sharp as the icicles on his eaves. He had a headnet on and eyephones pushed up on his forehead; clearly they had interrupted him in the midst of study.

"We're not pilgrims," Gabriel said just as Dominique was about to answer that they were. "We're here to visit the Institut."

"Ah. Traveling scholars," the man said with a skeptical lift of one eyebrow that meant he saw through them.

4

Gabriel took a gulp of coffee and said, "Don't you have any better books than this?"

"Oh, this is just the souvenir section," the man said wryly, handling a sample with a sunrise and flowers on the cover. "The real stuff is in the back. What are you interested in?"

"Everything," Gabriel said. "Complexity theory, no-etic architecture, metadynamics, that sort of thing."

"That should narrow it down to few million works. The recent classics are in the disk racks on the right wall. If you don't see what you want, tell the catalog. It'll suggest some titles. I can print up anything in about five minutes. Most of those works only come on spool or disk."

Gabriel disappeared into the back. The bookseller came forward to help himself to some coffee. "And what about you? What's your field of study?"

"Oh, I don't read," Dominique said.

The man blew on his coffee. "Ah. Not one of the 'truly conscious,' as they would say up on the mountain. The savants can afford to be snobs; they don't have to live in the real world where the literate are the oddities."

"There's no point in learning to read, unless you want to become a savant," Dominique said.

"And even then it can be a curse."

Dominique had often thought so but had never been tactless enough to say it aloud, especially in front of Gabriel. All the literate people he knew thought too much about themselves, always analyzing some inner person that others could never get to know. It made them seem hidden and secretive. In comparison, even women were easy to understand.

Gabriel came out again, looking overwhelmed.

"Too many choices?" the bookseller said.

"Oh no," Gabriel said hastily. "I suppose I could get all these in the Neige Valley, too, if only my mother's sysop weren't such a neanderthal."

The bookseller eyed him. "Which polity?"

"Allnet." Gabriel complained about it at least once a day, at home. Allnet was technical and business-focused, and had few of the subjects Gabriel wanted. "If I had any money I'd join Redpath. Actually, I've been on it already—day memberships from a friend."

"I may have met you then," the bookseller said. "What's your handle?"

"Really? You're a Redpath?" Gabriel looked at the man with new interest. "Did you vote in the last election, when Gröder got in? I would have voted for her."

"Don't tell them that on the mountain. They think we're all revolutionaries polluting the datastream."

"Do they give you any trouble?"

The bookseller gave a contemptuous laugh. "You talk as if they ever set foot down here. Everything they do is by DI remote. Virtual geology, virtual sociology. Why, if they left the Institut, they might have to look at something that doesn't fit the models. Like rocks or people."

In a disgruntled voice Gabriel said, "And they won't even let us have haptic interface technology."

"They've got better than that at Sorel. They've got DIs that transmit emotion."

"No!"

"Yes."

"I thought emotions were too complex."

"Well, it takes masses of processing power. More than you or I could afford."

"I suppose rational thought will be next."

Dominique's attention had begun to wander. He heard this kind of discussion all the time from Gabriel and his friends at home, and he found it hard to distinguish the

6

real information from the posturing and rhetoric. He stamped his feet to get the melting snow off.

"I think we're boring your illiterate friend," the bookseller said.

Gabriel flushed angrily; he never let his friends belittle Dominique. "Dominique's got a DI operator's license," he said sharply.

For a moment Dominique saw a flash of envy in the bookseller's eyes. It quickly disappeared behind an affectation of cynicism. "That fits the pattern. I daresay they don't let *you* have one," he said to Gabriel.

That hit too close to home. Wounded by the reminder, Gabriel said, "We'd better get going, Nika."

"Give my regards to the font of knowledge," the bookseller said.

They shouldered their packs and stepped out into the wind. They had been indoors just long enough to get sweaty and wet under their coats; the air felt twice as chilling.

"What a snob," Gabriel said as they headed down the street. "You'd think a Redpath would feel more solidarity with regular people."

Ahead was a large hotel, built to accommodate the summer crowds. "I suppose we'll be the only ones there," Dominique said.

"We're not stopping here," Gabriel said. His eyes were fixed tenaciously on the rock cliff at the end of the road.

"Oh, Gabriel!" Dominique groaned. "It can wait till morning. The Oracle isn't going away."

"I didn't bring enough money for a hotel," Gabriel said stiffly.

Dominique stopped in the road with the snow collecting on his eyebrows. Gabriel was supposed to be paying for all of this. "Then where are we going to stay? How are we going to buy a transport pass to get back?"

"I'm not going back," Gabriel said.

At last everything fell into place. Gabriel hadn't come to consult the Oracle at all. He had come in hopes of being selected as an acolyte at the Institut. What his radical friends didn't know was that Gabriel's disaffection was all personal, not political. He would give up all the ideology in the world to become a savant.

"You're crazy, Gabriel!" Dominique said. "They don't take people your age for acolytes. You would have to be trained from childhood to be a savant."

"I've trained myself," Gabriel said. "I've read, I've studied. All I've ever wanted is access to more information. I can do it."

"They won't care about that. People all over the world compete to get into the Institut Sorel. They only take the best."

Gabriel's voice was tense and high. "I'll make them measure my noetic potential. They'll see."

There was no arguing with him when his voice sounded like that. If Dominique persisted, it would only be harder for Gabriel to back down. Dominique tried to stifle his frustration. "Did you bring enough money for *me* to get back?"

"Call Mother for some credit," Gabriel said impatiently. He shifted his pack. "I'm going on up."

Dominique stood and watched his brother labor on down the buried street, his empty footsteps following. Gabriel hadn't brought enough money because he wanted to twist the arm of fate, to eliminate all other possibilities. But fate didn't work that way. As usual, Gabriel had set himself up for failure.

Gradually, Dominique's vexation faded. With a resigned certainty, he knew what was going to happen. Tomorrow morning Gabriel was going to come trudging back down that road from the Institut, rejected, his grandiose hopes in tatters. Then he would need someone friendly by him. Dominique couldn't leave his brother to face such a bruising alone.

When he caught up, Gabriel gave him a swift glance. "What are you doing?"

"I want to see the Oracle, too," Dominique lied.

Gabriel was too preoccupied to see through him.

The lights of the village ended where the black cliff began. Up the rock face a steep winding road ran, carved into the volcanic outcrop itself. Above the height of the village roofs the wind had scoured the road clean of snow. As he climbed, Dominique hugged the rock face, for the wind tugged as if to throw him off like a snowflake into the swirling void. Gabriel seemed energized by the proximity of his goal; he pushed on fast. His flashlight beam bobbed up the road ahead.

The road passed between two pillars of weathered rock and into an open courtyard. Only when he saw the windows did Dominique realize that he was surrounded not by the natural mountain, but by the buildings of the Institut. There was not a simple Euclidean shape in all the structures around him. No wall rose straight without fracturing into a thousand angles before it reached the roof. One artfully eroded spire was topped by antennas and a satellite dish. In a window high above, a single candle burned.

"Why would they use candles here, where they have all the most advanced technology in the world?" Dominique said.

"It must be symbolic; everything here is," Gabriel explained in a tense undertone. "It probably means they choose not to use all the technology they have. They are too wise to be ruled by machines, as pre-Renaissance people were."

Before them stood a shadowed, irregular arch where a towering door kept out the night.

"You'll have to have a question to get in," Gabriel said.

"What sort of question?"

"They only admit those who can puzzle the wise."

"I couldn't puzzle anyone here if I tried," Dominique said.

"Well, you'll have to, or wait outside all night."

There was no knob or catch, and they searched in vain for a bell or knocker. Frustrated, Gabriel finally shouted out, "Hello! Anyone there?" His voice echoed in the courtyard and died.

Dominique stamped his feet to remind them who was in charge. His breath blurred the air in front of him. At last a nearby shutter clattered open and an acolyte peered out. She wore a headnet on her shaved skull, with lowered eyephones that gave her a blank, inscrutable expression.

"You are being obvious," she said.

Gabriel whispered to Dominique, "Let me do the talking." Raising his voice, he said, "We've come to consult the Oracle."

"Are you riddles? Do you make the night wise?"

"We came all the way from the Neige Valley on foot. We nearly lost our way in the blizzard. You can't turn us back."

The acolyte looked into space, like someone watching a virtual scene. "Pilgrims," she said indifferently. "They say they walked here."

She listened a moment, then turned back. "What question will you give us?"

"You're no savant," Gabriel said. "Why should I tell you?"

Dominique stared at his brother, startled by his impudence. But the girl only shrugged and backed away from the window; a gray-haired woman in a high-collared saffron dhoura looked out. Her eyes were also masked behind the headnet visor. "Very well, puzzle me," she said.

Gabriel drew a tense breath, then said distinctly, "How close is the possible sphere?"

The savant laughed. "That's obvious. It's as close as your ear. Try again."

Gabriel licked his lips, disconcerted. He had obviously expected that one to work. But he had another ready. "Is it right to indict the mild mirage?"

This time the savant was silent, considering thoughtfully. At last she said, "That will be currency enough." She turned to Dominique. "And you?"

"Think of something," Gabriel hissed.

Apparently, they wanted gibberish. He had to pluck some disconnected words from his brain and wire them into a sentence. He stammered out, "Why does the secret candle cry?"

The savant frowned. "Are you sure it does?"

Dominique said, "You're being obvious."

The savant was silent for a very long time. At last she sighed and said, "Very well."

Dominique almost laughed. It was easier than he had thought to puzzle the wise.

Before them, an irregular crack split the massive door down the middle, and the two sides fell back into the wall. Automatic lights came on in the room beyond. Gabriel and Dominique stepped through, into the Institut Sorel.

🕯

From the windows of her chamber, the Voice of the Rinpoche of Sorel sometimes looked out on the sea, sometimes on the broad avenues of Paris or Abouta, or on the many other places the Institut monitored. Tonight the windows showed only the Vaudry Range, veiled by snow and night. The Voice sat cross-legged on her mat, her fingers in the jnana mudra, the headnet covering her skull.

In ages past, her ancestors had been Brahmins, statesmen and scholars; but she had shed all class and ethnicity in twenty-five years at Sorel. Her straight black hair was bobbed at the level of her jaw; she had not combed it in three days. Her eyes were darker than normal, puffy with grief.

As she stilled her concentration, the headnet wakened to the signal of alpha waves. The energies of the discontinuous interface focused on her optic nerve, and a vision floated before her. It was a visual metaphor of human civilization. It looked much like a landscape, which it was—the fitness landscape within which culture could continue to evolve and prosper. There was a plain on one side, a range of mountains on the other: Oracle's heuristic representation of the stable and chaotic states. A path snaked along the edge of the mountain range, sometimes forking, sometimes whole. Branches that dipped too far into the rough topology of chaos usually disappeared or looped back into the changeless plain of stability. With a finger the Voice traced the middle course, the one that balanced just on the edge, in the terrain of complexity. In that narrow ribbon lay the path of maximum fitness, where extinction events and leaps of adaptation were part of the mathematics of existence.

The Voice focused on the edge of the graph, where the landscape ended in a blank cliff. As she swooped lower with a speed that would have given anyone else vertigo, the seeming simplicity of the model dissolved. The path of civilization parted into a myriad of intertwined threads over a rugged hodgepodge of hills and craters. She focused on one of the threads till it, too, resolved into an intricate, twining rope of variants wound around a central strand. That strand represented the cultural matrix where Sorel lay. If she had gone down in scale by more orders of magnitude, she could have resolved the graph to the very level of individual savants' work. Few places on earth were scrutinized as closely as Sorel.

At the edge of the chasm where the data ended, she commanded Oracle to construct a hypothetical future. Gray hills and valleys appeared where all had been blank, and Sorel's path snaked forward, then veered sharply into the domain of chaos. Frowning, the Rinpoche's Voice ordered the assumptions changed, and a new landscape built itself. This time the Institut's line careened off into the plain.

She opened her eyes and the display disappeared. She rose from her mat and went to the window where the blustery snow traced wild paths on the air. The courtyard and Institut buildings looked solid and stable in comparison. It was an illusion, of course: rock was merely a snowstorm on another scale.

Oracle had been showing omens of instability for months now. She had seen it in other cultural lines, but none had ever given her such unease. This time, change would affect Sorel; and as Sorel went, so went a good part of human civilization.

"Naidu?"

The uncertain footsteps, the wavering voice, made her close her eyes for a moment, wishing the present away. When she turned, the old man was standing in the doorway.

"Go back to bed, Rinpoche," she said. "You should be asleep."

"Why? What time is it?" he said, rubbing his forehead anxiously.

His obsession with time was a new aspect of his growing dementia. As memory left him, so did the capacity to judge the passage of time. The gridwork of sequence had collapsed upon him, making all events equally near, equally far. Though he could not say so, it clearly terrified him. He slept with a watch clutched in his hand.

Naidu crossed the darkened room. His watery eyes fastened on her headnet, and he said, "Is that mine?"

"No, cheri, it's mine," she said.

"Where is my DI? There's something I need you to do."

"I'll do it tomorrow. There will be time."

They had had to take his equipment away. The last few times he had tried to operate her had been too agonizing. She had had to share his wandering thoughts, his confusion, his childlike rage. It had been so unlike the Rinpoche she had served—and loved—for fifteen years. As his Voice, she had known his deep reasoning, his unfailing moral core, from the inside. His mind had been one of immense clarity, honed by a lifetime of training, perfectly suited to lead Sorel. They had compared him to Aquinas and Bourassa. She had been his eyes on the outside world and had thus collaborated in the masterwork of his leadership.

"I shall become an organism once again and know life uncontaminated by mind," he had said in a lucid moment when it first became clear that the usual cures were not going to work on him, that there was still something about the human brain that even Sorel didn't know.

He still looked like that person, though somehow slacker, less animate. She knew she ought to love this body, this organism, for the man who had once inhabited it, but all she could feel was disgust at it for having betrayed him.

He fussed a little about going back to bed, but she finally got him to lie down and switched on the hypnotic display they had installed on his ceiling to keep him calm. When she returned to the outer chamber, the snowstorm had intensified; ice crystals ticked against the window-panes. The room felt cold.

Very few people in Sorel, and no one outside, knew of the Rinpoche's condition. They were training another Rinpoche, but he was only seven years old. In the meantime, they could only guess at what their beloved leader would have done. In all of Sorel's history, there had never been a worse time for the crisis Oracle was predicting.

The few savants who knew the situation would often say to her, "You knew his mind better than anyone; you shared it. You must know what he would do." And gradually, from telling them her best guesses, she had grown in their eyes—she, a mere parlant, no more than a body trained to house another's mind. She knew nothing of leadership, yet now learned people deferred to her. She would have traded it all away to feel his firm mind guiding her.

She closed her eyes again, and the graph appeared in the air. This time she gave the Rinpoche's private access code and called up the detail of the Institut's inner workings. She searched for instabilities, straining the graph's strands one by one. The savants all thought the imbalance was societal, but she could not shake the feeling that the crisis would come from within.

That did not simplify the problem. Sorel was a society in itself, complex with history. It was the oldest of the great institutes founded at the beginning of the third millenium. In that era, the mechanistic sciences that had briefly seduced humanity with their technological prowess had dissolved into conflicting sects, all claiming to have the true key to reality. The old sciences, blinded by their materialism, counted as "real" only what could be detected or measured, which limited reality to matter, energy, space, and time. Pattern was merely a property of these. But in the Renaissance Dernier scholars discovered the crucial nonmaterial constituent—information. Soon matter, energy, space, and time were seen as mere properties of information.

No longer would researchers spend their efforts dissecting things to learn how they ran; instead, they would compute the governing algorithms that gave all things their shape and structure. They would leave the material and delve into the real.

For centuries, Sorel had been the world center of information mechanics. In these irregular buildings, savants had mapped the mathematics of epidemics and rumor propagation. They had unlocked the metadynamics of economies and population growth and the fitness landscapes of nation-states. As the principles of social ecology emerged, humankind could finally hope to graph its way to a world without eruptions of disorder like poverty, crime, or war. Even now, after centuries, civilization was still (as the mathematics said it must be) a balancing act—but because of Sorel it was no longer a blind blunder.

The Rinpoche's Voice sighed and cut off the display, gazing out into the snowy courtyard. The Rinpoche had loved Sorel, and for him she loved it, too. She hoped she would not live to see it threatened.

🕯

The room the two pilgrims entered was the most distracting space Dominique had ever seen. The red glowing ceiling was not a surface but an intricately coved and recoved three-dimensional fractal. In places you could see deep into the recesses of the pattern, where the color became profound as wine; in others, the self-repeating cavities devolved quickly into the texture of sponge. Connecting ceiling to floor was a forest of glowing cords of every dimension, from microfilament to thick optical cable. Their colors changed in waves, beckoning the visitors forward.

The savant from the window was standing beyond the forest of lightfibers, her eyeshades blank as eggs. As the two pilgrims came up, she said, "Our building is an allegory. Acolytes contemplate it for many years until they discover the principles it signifies."

She paused. Unfathomable thoughts seemed to populate the silence. "I cannot promise that Oracle can answer your questions. But in every situation, unpredictability exists. Come with me."

Beyond the first room, the floor fell away, and they found themselves threading single file across a transparent bridge above an upside-down room. Somehow, the curtains hung erect below them. Candles burned in sconces, their flames rising serenely downward. For a dizzying moment Dominique had the feeling that he was the one reversed and wanted to turn his head around. Gabriel pushed him on.

On the other side they came to an octagonal room with doors in each wall. In the center was an eight-sided settee with all seats facing outward. The savant said, "You may wait here. I will seek the voyant."

Nervously, Gabriel asked, "Will it be Voyant Raspail?"

The savant's face was uncommunicative. "She is the only voyant we have."

She stepped into a framed painting, and disappeared.

Dominique threw himself down on the settee, but Gabriel paced nervously.

"Voyant Raspail!" he said, his voice hushed as if someone might be listening. "Dominique, do you know what that means?"

"What?"

"She is the greatest voyant who has ever lived. In the last few years there has been a series of amazing discoveries out of Sorel. I can't explain them; it's too complicated. But they say there is another great paradigm shift coming, a breakthrough in our understanding of the world. And it's all due to Raspail."

"And she will tell our fortunes?" Dominique asked skeptically.

"Oh don't be such an idiot!" Gabriel exclaimed. "The Oracle will give us an extremely sophisticated aptitude test. We'll find out what we're good for."

"I know what I'm good for."

"Well, I don't."

They waited in silence for a long time. The air was still chill; Dominique noticed that the snow on his pack had not melted. At last the savant emerged from one of the doors.

"Oracle is ready for you," she said. "Which of you wishes to go first?"

"Me!" Gabriel nearly shouted. "Me," he said again, in a controlled voice.

The savant gestured him through the door.

Alone, Dominique paced, trying to warm up. At last, curious, he opened one of the doors. Beyond was a long hallway lined with doors. Simultaneously, dozens of Dominiques opened the doors all down the hall and stared back at him. He hastily closed it again.

Presently the savant came out from yet another door. "We are ready for you," she said.

"I don't really need this, if it's any trouble," he said.

She stared at him in such a way that he meekly went where she pointed.

The room beyond was completely dark. When he stepped forward, the touch of his foot set off a reaction in the floor, and azure galaxies swirled away from his glowing footprint. By its light he saw that he was at the base of a spiral ramp. He followed the ramp up, treading on sparks and hurricanes. At the apex a chair stood, reflected in the polished floor as if floating in still water. Dropping his pack, he gingerly sat down.

The light faded. He turned around and saw, hanging in the air behind him, a bubble of distortion, like a spherical heat wave. It could only be one thing: a discontinuous interface like the ones the headnets created to feed information directly to the optic nerve. But those were microscopic; this one was big enough to encompass an entire brain.

It moved slowly toward him. He drew away, unnerved.

"Sit back, please," a voice said.

Reluctantly, he turned around and settled back against the headrest, clutching the chair arms. Thousands of people had done this without any harm.

Merging with the DI bubble was like sinking past the surface of a lake. Lights traced fireworks across his vision—at first senseless, then resolving into a pattern of fishes sporting in a rainbow sea. He watched, intrigued, then realized he was beginning to see a hidden, three-dimensional image. As he gazed into it, he found himself standing inside a massive cathedral dome with sunlight pouring through a window in the ceiling; yet the sporting fishes were still there. As he moved he brushed something and realized there was another image hidden under this one—a tactile image. He raised his hands to feel it, but then the vision ceased.

When he returned to the waiting room, Gabriel was sitting on the settee, chin on his fists. Dominique sat down beside him. "It was beautiful," he said.

"What was?"

"The Oracle. Didn't you think so?"

"All I saw was some lights."

They waited in silence.

19

The savant stood before them. "Gabriel," she said, though the brothers had never mentioned their names. Gabriel jumped up and went through the door she indicated. "Dominique," she said, and pointed to another door. "The Rinpoche has asked to see you."

Surprise stopped him cold. The Rinpoche? What would an enlightened being want with him?

The figure at the other end of the long room was larger than human scale; his head nearly brushed the tall ceiling. Feeling dwarfed, Dominique forced himself forward. After several steps he realized that he was growing, or the room was shrinking around him. It was all a trick of distorted perspective. With another three steps he grew a foot and saw that the person waiting was merely a small, dark-skinned woman with bobbed black hair. No one superhuman. Not the Rinpoche at all.

When he came to a halt before her, she smiled, but the expression looked sad on her face. "Dominique," she said, "I am the Voice of the Rinpoche of Sorel."

He had to force himself not to draw back. It *was* the Rinpoche, in a way. The woman was a parlant: she was transmitting to the Rinpoche all she witnessed, and he controlled all she said and did, when he chose. Dominique couldn't meet her eyes without wondering who he was seeing: herself or the puppeteer controlling her from outside. But they said you could never tell the difference. He realized he was staring and looked down self-consciously.

"Oracle's reading of your noetic pattern was very interesting," she said, and held out on her hand a small crystal globe enclosing what seemed to be a dandelion puff. He looked at it, then at her again.

"Do you know what this is?"

"No."

"It is a diatom graph. The best representation we have found for a human mind. Each mind has a characteristic fingerprint, a habitual way of working. We call it noetic architecture. Of course, this model is vastly simplified. But it is your diatom graph."

Intrigued, Dominique took it from her hand and turned it around in his. Inside the glass was a tiny sphere of colored branches, all radiating from the center in an intricate network. "So it was just a brain scan Oracle did?" he asked.

"No. A brain scan maps neurons. The diatom graph shows the informational patterns of brain functions. You see, it is not the neurons that make us human. It is their rules of organization. You might say this is a picture of consciousness."

"It's very beautiful," Dominique said.

"That is no coincidence. What we call aesthetics is only our way of perceiving high levels of informational organization. In this universe, information is always growing more complex. And as it grows complex, it grows more beautiful."

"Can I keep it?" Dominique said.

"No, I will need it a little while longer."

He gave it back to her. She held it up to the light, studying it. "How does it happen that you never learned to read?"

Startled, Dominique said, "You can tell that?"

"Oh, yes. Literacy creates a fundamental change in brain functions, a characteristic trace on the diatom graph. Yours shows no hint of it."

"I really didn't need it," he said. "All I do is make and repair seismic monitors. If there are any instructions, the processor reads them or shows me."

"That is very lucky for us," the Rinpoche's Voice said.

"What?"

She smiled at him, but this time he had the feeling the smile was coming from far away. "The graph shows you have an aptitude that would have been spoiled if you had learned to read. Most people don't know it, but literacy can actually make a person less suited for certain tasks."

"Like what?" Dominique said.

Instead of answering, she said, "We practice two sorts of training here at Sorel. One is the analytical model, in which our acolytes learn to divide and classify. Rationality is segregated from fantasy, thought from feeling, desire from discipline. It is a process full of polar opposites, and from it our savants emerge. You will never be a savant."

Dominique laughed. "I didn't need Oracle to tell me that. Gabriel's the smart one in the family."

"But there is another sort of training. In it, intuition and synthesis are the goals. We teach these acolytes no analysis. They learn sensory and spatial skills. Dream, desire, and reason are integrally connected. It enables them to make intuitive leaps and grasp whole pictures. These are the acolytes who become our voyants. That is what we wish you to be."

There was a silence as Dominique slowly absorbed what she was saying. He felt like a gyroscope that had suddenly stopped spinning. "A voyant?" he stammered. "Me?"

A note of urgency crept into her voice. "Noetic patterns like yours are extremely rare and getting rarer. Normally, we would not accept an applicant older than five or six years. But our situation has become an emergency. We have only one voyant. You would become apprentice to Raspail."

"Hold on," Dominique said. This was going too fast.

"Yes?" the Voice said.

"What *is* a voyant, anyway?"

If she was surprised at the question, she didn't show it. "Oracle creates graphs so complex that no screen or hologram can display them whole. The only screen Oracle can draw on is the human brain itself. Humans are still the ideal decoders."

"So that's what the voyant is? The screen?"

"In a manner of speaking. Voyants' brains are specially designed to receive and sort enormous amounts of information."

"And you think I could do it?"

"I don't think. I know."

Gabriel wouldn't believe it. Plain, predictable Dominique, the brother without the brains, wanted by the savants of Sorel. Dominique nearly laughed at the thought of telling his brother the unlikely news; then, as the scenario took on more reality, his thoughts skidded to a halt. Gabriel would be furious. And what would his mother do? It was impossible; his life was built on a scaffold of obligations.

"It's really nice of you—" he began.

"Let me show you something," the Rinpoche's Voice broke in. She stepped back, and Dominique saw in the shadows behind her a cylindrical holo vitrine. She typed quickly into its keyboard, and an image appeared.

On the floor of the vitrine was a heap of bright yellow symbols shaped like jacks but moving like tiny bugs. As Dominique watched, they milled around; finally, out of the disordered heap grew a structure a little like a honeycomb. Then, as Dominique was just about to conclude that the show was over, the honeycomb abruptly collapsed and the bugs went into a flurry of activity. Presently another structure emerged, reaching higher toward the middle of the vitrine. This time multiple honeycombs were built into interlocking towers and cross-braces.

"You can watch it for hours," the Rinpoche's Voice said, "and the same events recur, but never in the same way. Each time a state of order is reached, it persists for a while, then collapses and reforms in a state of higher complexity."

"Oh," Dominique said.

"I am showing you this so you will understand how important it is for you to stay here. This model demonstrates a principle we call self-organized criticality. A system with this property exhibits long periods of stasis followed by bursts of rapid change. Many complex systems show this kind of behavior. Biological evolution, for example. Also economies, cultures, and nation-states. All dynamic systems, left to themselves, tend toward greater order and organization. Ecosystems evolve toward a state of perfect balance, cultures toward equilibrium. At last, each system will become deadlocked in a state of advanced efficiency. This is called an 'order crisis.' The system becomes so perfectly adapted that it cannot change or grow. Eventually, the slightest change results in a spontaneous outbreak of randomness in which order collapses into creative inefficiency again. In both biology and history, mass extinction results—in the one, extinction of species, in the other, extinction of cultures and ideas. But once complexity is re-established, so is flexibility and growth. It is impossible to predict what type of change will occur, but that it *will* occur is mathematically certain.

"One of our savants, who studies our present society, believes we have been locked in an order crisis since the middle of the third millenium. She is convinced we are on the brink of a phase transition into a period of chaos that will result, eventually, in a new and higher level of order. Whether this is good or bad is a subject of great debate among the savants. Regardless, it is highly probable that Sorel will be in the midst of this change. In fact, the pebble that starts the avalanche may be here, anywhere around us."

The shifting light from another breakdown of order in the holo vitrine reflected on her face as she looked seriously at Dominique. "The whole world is about to change, Dominique. The work we do here may determine the course of that change. We need you for that work to continue."

He thought of home, and the Neige Valley, and his friends. How permanent and trustworthy it had always seemed. If the savants were right, then all the obligations tying him to home might cease to exist.

All he had done was come to keep Gabriel company in a crazy quest. He had never even wanted Oracle to tell his future. Now it seemed his future would be changed no matter what. For a moment he wished he had never come. He had been happy in his ignorance.

"You have to stay, you see," the Rinpoche's Voice said.

"What if I can't do the work?" Dominique protested weakly.

"You can."

"You sound pretty sure."

"I've never seen a diatom graph I was surer of."

"Well, all right," Dominique said. "Maybe for a while." She smiled. "Welcome to Sorel, Dominique Cadot."

The Rinpoche's Voice held out her hand again; this time, in it was a small crystal chip. "Take it," she said.

Dominique picked it up. It was a communication device of some sort.

"I must ask one more thing of you," she said. "We know that Sorel is balanced on the edge of change; we do not know what the trigger will be. We are all inside the pattern; it is difficult for us to see it. As Raspail's apprentice, you will have access to many things going on at the Institut. Watch for the random factor. Let me know where it is, if you see it. Press your thumb against the crystal now."

He did as she said. Nothing happened.

"Good," she said. "Now it will respond only to you. If you wish to communicate with me, press your thumb against it again. I will know you have found something."

She took the chip from his hand, peeled off an adhesive backing, then said, "Turn around." When he did, she placed the chip behind his ear and pressed it to his skull. Startled, he felt it with a finger. "For safekeeping," she explained. "Don't worry, it's waterproof."

"Now you must meet Raspail," she said. "Please don't tell her about the chip."

Dominique forced himself not to finger the device any more. It made him vaguely uneasy to have something to hide from his tutor, as if he had been commanded to spy on her.

Across the room the door opened, and a tall woman entered. Her citrine academic gown looked hastily thrown on over a plain gray dhoura. As she crossed the distorted room, seeming to cover yards with each step, Dominique watched her face. It reminded him of Mont Chatoyer: raw contours made beautiful by the insults of time. Her grey-silver hair was cropped close; her slightly slanting eyes had deep lines beneath them.

She came to a halt before the Rinpoche's Voice. "Raspail, this is Dominique," the Voice said in a calm tone. "He has agreed to become your apprentice."

The voyant glanced at him, and muscles tightened in her face. "You can't saddle me with another assignment now," she said in a low, tense voice.

"He is not an assignment; he is an opportunity. You have seen his diatom graph."

"Yes," she admitted reluctantly. "Can't we send him to another institute?"

"No. We need him here. We need *you* to train him, Raspail."

For an instant Raspail closed her eyes as if to withdraw from the conversation; when she opened them again they were burning. "Have you told him the truth about the training?"

"What is the truth?"

Raspail turned on Dominique fiercely. "Becoming a voyant is hard. Harder than anything you can imagine. You must give up all that you think of as your self. There is no way to survive it without fire inside. There can be nothing in your heart but the will to be a voyant."

The Rinpoche's Voice said calmly, "And yet people have been doing it for three centuries."

The voyant was trying to scare him off, though he didn't know why. Dominique might not have had fire inside, but he also didn't scare easily. "I've done hard things before," he said.

Her expression was as dismissive as Gabriel's. He felt tired of always being discounted. He wanted to prove that she was wrong about him.

"Try it, Raspail," the Rinpoche's Voice said.

For a moment the voyant stood like an embattled spire defying entropy, too stubborn to fall. Then her stiff shoulders twitched in what might have been a shrug.

The Voice turned to Dominique. "Wait in the antechamber for a moment."

When Dominique reached the eight-sided waiting room, he found Gabriel standing there, hands stuffed in his pockets, brows boxing one another. "This was a total farce," he said. "They couldn't tell me a damned thing I didn't already know. So much for the Oracle; I could have gotten better advice from a fortune teller. Let's go."

So they hadn't offered him a place as an acolyte. "Gabriel—" Dominique started.

"It was just a character analysis, no guidance. It didn't settle anything."

"Gabriel, I'm not going back. You've got to tell Mother."

Slowly, Gabriel focused on him. "What?"

"They offered me an apprenticeship. To work with the voyant." In the face of Gabriel's disappointment, Dominique felt obscurely ashamed.

Gabriel's eyes widened as he saw his brother in a new light—the light of his own failure. "Here? A voyant?"

"It's only till they find out I can't do the work." Dominique tried to grin. "Listen, can I send you a message at the hotel tomorrow?"

"No. No, I'm not waiting around." Gabriel started off stiffly toward the entrance. "Enjoy your life," he said bitterly over his shoulder.

"It's not my fault, Gabriel!" Dominique called after him.

Gabriel didn't pause. Dominique stood, half furious, half hurt, unsure whether to go after him. A hand touched his shoulder. He looked around to find Raspail at his side.

"Let him go," she said softly.

"But he's my brother!" Dominique said.

"You have lost him," Raspail said. "He is just the first of many things. You will have to learn to lose, and lose, and lose, if you want to be a voyant."

The words were harsh, but there was a furtive compassion in her voice, a human face frozen under ice. He sensed that she was talking about herself, and not him at all.

The moment was gone; now she was tense and stern again. Saying, "Come," she started toward one of the doors. Dominique glanced one last time after Gabriel, then followed her.

There was a maze of corridors. Voyant Raspail's pace picked up, till she was striding on ahead of Dominique. Down a long, dimly lit passage lined with doors her footsteps echoed impatiently. When she reached an enameled doorway she jerked it open and plunged through, into a comfortable apartment. Dominique stood in the doorway, still breathless from the walk, feeling unwelcome and uncertain what to do. Preoccupied, Raspail threw her gloves on a table, then without a word crossed to a bedroom door and slammed it behind her.

In the silence Dominique realized that someone else was sitting across the room in the darkened window seat with a book on his lap, staring at Dominique with wide and startled eyes.

"Hello," Dominique said awkwardly. "My name's Dominique."

"I am Aristide," the other said. As he set the book aside, Dominique saw that he had not been reading, but tearing the pages into intricate patterns. Aristide stood, brushing a snowfall of shredded paper onto the floor, then approached cautiously.

He was about Dominique's height, but thin as a mannikin of twisted wire. His dark eyes looked huge in his pale face. Neglected curls of black hair fell in his eyes. "What do you want?" he said.

"I guess this is where they want me to stay," Dominique said, shifting his pack. It was beginning to feel heavy.

Aristide had an intense, unblinking gaze. "These are the voyant's chambers," he said.

"I know."

"Who told you to come here?"

"The Rinpoche's Voice. Listen, I don't want to barge in. Why don't I just go tell them this isn't working out?" He began to back away.

"No!" Suddenly, Aristide's hand shot out to stop him. His eyes searched Dominique's face for the truth. "They really sent you here? They'll let me keep you?"

Laughing to cover his confusion, Dominique said, "I guess so."

A smile lit Aristide's face. It seemed to brighten the whole room. "Come in!" he said excitedly.

Feeling welcome for the first time since setting foot in Sorel, Dominique stepped in.

A second look around revealed the eccentricity of the room. On one table, a huge multicolored mound of candle wax dripped from the edge onto the floor, studded with bits of shiny foil and surmounted by two wings broken from a ceramic angel. The carpet had been carefully unraveled on one side and rewoven to climb the wall in purple tendrils on the other.

"Does this place ever get normal?" Dominique said, rubbing his eyes wearily.

"Do you like to eat?" Aristide asked intently.

"Are you kidding?" Dominique's stomach growled at the thought.

"Good! We can order some food." He took Dominique's arm and dragged him into the kitchen.

The table was occupied by a tangled tower of interlocking forks. "Don't touch it, it's for Raspail," Aristide said. He then produced a well-thumbed menu for the autoserver.

Dominique liked to cook almost as much as he liked to eat. He was soon able to select enough raw ingredients for a decent paella. A little more hunting revealed a pan. Aristide had gotten distracted among the dishes. As Dominique began to chop vegetables, Aristide took two overturned cups and made one chase another across the counter. One of the cups was yipping.

This was not how Dominique had imagined the brilliant savants spending their time. "So, where are you from, Aristide?" he asked.

The cups paused and turned to look at him, their handles turned up inquisitively. "From?" Aristide said as if the word were nonsense. The cups turned and raced thumpingly over to the cutting board, where they sniffed garlic, then shook in delight.

"Your home. You know, where does your family live?"

Aristide pushed a handful of black hair out of his eyes. "Oh. I don't know."

"You must have come here pretty young, then."

Aristide smiled craftily. "I didn't come here. I was made here. Raspail invented me."

He fitted two salt dishes over his eyes and coffee mugs over his hands, then began to walk around the kitchen stiff-limbed and stub-armed, like a mechanical man from an ancient cinema. Dominique laughed. But a footstep from the bedroom next door made Aristide quickly drop the act and whisk the dishes back into the cupboard. He perched innocently on the counter. "She doesn't like me to wear the crockery," he confided in a whisper.

"What exactly do you do around here, Aristide?" Dominique asked, dumping oil into the pan.

Aristide stared as if he'd asked the purpose of the floor. "I am Raspail's apprentice."

"Oh, really? I didn't know she had one already. That's what I'm going to be."

"You?" Aristide looked as if he couldn't decide whether to collapse in laughter.

"That's what they tell me."

A thought occurred to Aristide; as it crossed his face, it wiped out the laughter. "Is this because of what I did yesterday?" he said.

"I don't know. What did you do yesterday?"

"I imploded a datamass. It was just a fluke, a backwash in the processing flow. I didn't do it on purpose." He looked at Dominique apprehensively. "It was Savant Barrère's. She's working on historical dynamics and the coming phase transition. Have you heard of it?"

"I think so."

Aristide leaned close and whispered, "I wiped out all her data. We don't know if she has a copy. Raspail hasn't dared to ask her yet."

Dominique paused, spoon in hand. The paella sizzled in the pan. "That sounds kind of serious," he said.

Aristide began to laugh uproariously. "The savants are going to slit my throat when they find out." He sobered abruptly. "They don't know yet, do they?"

"I don't know. I don't think it has anything to do with my being here."

Nevertheless, Aristide fell silent and thoughtful. Dominique dished up two plates of food. He wolfed down two helpings, standing at the counter, while Aristide toyed unhungrily with his. Glancing across the stove, Dominique noticed how delicate Aristide's hands were—fragile and fine, as if blown out of milky, translucent glass. He looked up and found the apprentice watching him. He smiled, but Aristide crossed his arms defensively to hide his hands.

"What kind of work does an apprentice voyant do?" Dominique asked.

"Didn't they tell you?"

"Voyant Raspail tried. All she could say was how hard it was. I figured she was trying to scare me away."

Aristide paused. "If I answered, you would think I was trying to scare you as well."

"Just tell me what it's like to operate the Oracle."

Aristide's eyes looked past Dominique, toward some horizon that wasn't there. "You should ask what it's like *not* to operate Oracle. Compared to Oracle, everything else is like being a fish in muddy water. All you know is upstream and downstream. There is no sky, no landscape, only murk."

"So you think I ought to stay?"

Aristide turned eyes oddly drained of emotion on him. In a flat voice, he said, "If I were you, I would get out of here as fast as I could, and run till they could never find me again."

Dominique was no longer hungry. He put down his fork to study Aristide, wondering what he meant. "But you're still here," he said.

"I said if I were you."

They said little after that. Aristide went back out into the living room and set to work shredding his book again. Dominique wandered around, yawning hugely. At last he said, "Where do you want me to sleep?"

"There's an extra bed in my room," Aristide said, and got up to show him.

It turned out to be no more than a cot, but Dominique gratefully tossed his pack under it, then tossed himself on top.

There was a nightstand between the beds, placed against the window, and on it burned a candle with a glass hurricane shade over it. Dominique stared at it, in his drowsiness struggling to grasp a revelation he felt ought to be there.

"I know," he said. "We saw that candle earlier tonight, when we came up the road to Sorel. I asked Gabriel why anyone would want to light a candle here."

"Dominique," Aristide said seriously, "Do dogs fall in love?"

Dominique was too sleepy to make sense of that. "I don't know," he said.

But as soon as he burrowed under the pile of quilts and lay still, sleep eluded him. All that had happened kept swirling through his mind.

When he turned to look, Aristide was lying on his bed, head propped on his fist, watching the candle. Its yellow flame cast a gentle light on his face. He looked pensive, as if remembering something from long ago. "Why do you light it?" Dominique said at last.

"Down in the east wing they teach the acolytes to model flames in mathematics," Aristide said.

"Did you learn to do that?" Dominique asked.

"No. I was never an acolyte. They couldn't let me learn to read. But I have seen the mathematics modeled by Oracle. I have seen a flame created from formulas instead of wax. At this scale it looks simple, but on the molecular level it's incredibly turbulent. The surface is wrinkly, and inside it's all stretched and distorted. Did you know that a flame is the opposite of a living thing?"

"No."

"It's an information-conversion system, just like a plant or a person. But instead of building patterns, as life will, it destroys them. It's a little pocketful of entropy."

Those were the last words Dominique heard before drifting off to sleep.

Later that night he roused long enough to see that the candle had burned down to a stub. He reached out to snuff it, but Aristide lunged out and caught his wrist in a steely grip. "Don't touch it," he said through clenched teeth.

"Sorry," Dominique stammered. "I thought you were asleep."

As he tried to fall asleep again, he could see the glint of Aristide's eyes watching him from out of the darkness.

Chapter 2

When Sorel slept, Oracle still woke. Quiet atop its mountain peak, the unsleeping witness watched the galaxies, listened to the wind, measured the grinding motion of the earth underneath, always searching for pattern. But like its Delphic namesake, all its information was useless until someone asked it the right question. Oracle did not draw conclusions. It drew pictures.

Dominique woke with a stripe of sunlight lying across his face. Aristide was a motionless lump in the opposite bed. When Dominique turned onto his back, he saw what he had missed the night before: the ceiling above him was a collage of glass bottles shattered at the necks. Their bases were glued to the ceiling, sharp edges pointing down. The sunlight winked off them, tossing wild spectra around the room: ruby, jade, peacock, sapphire. Dominique didn't feel easy till he had gotten out from under them.

When he came into the living room, he found Voyant Raspail sitting in the window seat, studying the book Aristide had demolished the night before. She finished dictating into a recorder, then paused to take a photo of a damaged page.

"So you are still here," she said. When she looked up, her face was austere, as if marshalled tight against despondence. Dominique wondered how anyone so successful could seem so unhappy.

"Where did you sleep?" she asked.

"Aristide's room."

"What did Aristide say?"

"He was very nice." Dominique's instinct was not to say much till he knew what was going on. "No one mentioned you already had an apprentice."

"No. They wouldn't." Her voice was flat as rolled metal. "There are many bright people here at Sorel, but not many kind ones. From your graph, I think kindness is something you have."

His mother had always teased him about being the one in the family who looked after stray animals and idiots. Meaning Gabriel, of course. He had never mentally translated that into "kindness," but the word certainly didn't offend him.

"Look after him, will you?" Raspail said softly.

There was a silence. At last Dominique said, "I'm sure Aristide doesn't need my protection."

"Oh, yes he does," Raspail whispered.

"From what?"

"From Sorel."

She rose, and her voice turned neutral. "What's your background? Do you know how to use a headnet?"

"Of course," Dominique said. What was she thinking? Everyone knew how to use headnets.

"A DI helmet?"

"Yes. I got a license to use them in my work."

"Remote manipulation?"

Dominique wrinkled his nose in distaste. "Sometimes." Often, actually. When hardware in the field broke or needed a skilled overhaul, he usually linked up with someone on the spot via the DI helmet. It fed him their perceptions and allowed him to manipulate their hands and eyes. The transmission was expensive, but not as expensive as going there in the flesh. He had never gotten used to the feeling of operating someone else, or being operated himself. "I think it's creepy," he said.

"A common reaction," Raspail said. "You will have to overcome it."

There was a stumble of bare feet behind them. Aristide came from the bedroom, still punching his way out of a cocoon of fatigue. When he saw them he froze, eyes shifting apprehensively from one to the other.

Raspail went to him. A few feet away, she held out her hand, elbow crooked as if to arm-wrestle in the air. He took the challenge, and for a few moments they held a mock-competition, straining against one another. Aristide finally won, and Raspail put an arm around his shoulder and pulled him close to kiss his forehead. Then she turned away toward the window, the remote scholar again.

A revelation hit Dominique: They loved each other. Raspail was trying not to show it, but there had been a bright, brief flash of joy out of the grayness when she had seen Aristide.

This is going to be complicated, Dominique thought.

"Tea?" Aristide asked him.

"Sure," he said and followed into the kitchen.

They sat around the kitchen table, from which the fork sculpture had mysteriously disappeared. Aristide played with his paper napkin, folding it into complicated shapes. Raspail stared, preoccupied, into her teacup.

"We need to work on Barrère's project today," she said.

Aristide glanced at her through dark hair.

"I recorded a pattern just before pulling you out of that feedback loop. Do you remember it?"

Aristide shook his head, staring at his napkin, which was now shaped like a crab. When he looked up, Dominique saw dread in his eyes.

Persuasively, Raspail said, "If it is what I think, no one will even notice a little lost data. But you need to look at it."

Aristide began slowly pulling the legs off the crab.

"Can I see it, too?" Dominique asked.

From the voyant's look he knew he had said something ridiculous. She seemed to be searching for a way to break it to him kindly. "If you were to enter Oracle's processing flow without training, and were lucky, you would see nothing. If you were unlucky, the chances are good that the information load would incinerate your brain. The graphic we are working on is drawn on a five-dimensional manifold. Can you even imagine four dimensions? Think of the three you know, then try to picture a fourth axis projecting at a right angle to all the others."

Dominique tried, then shook his head. Raspail said, "It is impossible without Oracle's help. Oracle lets us perceive dimensions we cannot even imagine otherwise. But it takes years of practice to do it safely."

"Let him see Oracle, at least," Aristide suggested suddenly.

"I saw it last night," Dominique said.

Raspail laughed. "What you saw was—how shall I put it? A church, a theater. A drama of lights and echoes they call Oracle. The savants had it built to impress the pilgrims in reward for their donations. The real Oracle is in this wing." She rose. "Come with us."

She led the way out of the apartment into the corridor of endless doors. The fourth on the left, indistinguishable from all the others, was the one she chose. Inside was an airlock, and beyond that two more dust-seal doors that finally opened onto a curving ramp that led gently downward. The air was odorless and quiet.

Dominique drew close to Aristide as Raspail strode on ahead. "Thanks," he said quietly. "I was afraid she wasn't going to let me get near Oracle."

"You were *near* it last night," Aristide said. "Our apartment is built into the side of it."

"You mean—"

"We're inside it now."

They had begun to pass doorways to right and left. There was a slight hum from the air conditioning. Raspail slowed her pace and said, "These are the entrances to specialized control chambers. Most have been added in the past 180 years, as we learned to use Oracle for different purposes."

"What sort of purposes?" Dominique asked.

"Basal lattices, Weisman nets, filicology."

Only the last made any sense to Dominique. "Study of ferns? You have a special room for that?"

"Study of fernlike information structures," Raspail said patiently.

"Do you have to know all those disciplines?"

"Ideally, we would have a voyant specializing in each. We used to. When I was an apprentice there was a team of voyants, and these control rooms were busy round the clock. These days, we are just muddling through."

She drew ahead again. Aristide whispered, "Don't worry, you don't need to know all the disciplines. Sometimes the savants don't even tell us what their projects are about; they just give us the data to play with."

As the ramp spiraled deeper into Oracle's throat, Dominique felt around him a presence, watching. Uneasily, he asked, "Does Oracle have a brain?"

"It is not aware, if that is what you mean," Raspail said without turning.

The rampway ended in the last control booth. As they entered, the lights and instrument panel came on automatically. The room was domed and circular, lined with screens and equipment except on the far right, where a section of photonic processors had been removed to make space for a small glassblower's furnace and marble-topped work table, now cluttered with tongs, crucibles, and a stack of glass rods.

In the center of the room stood two reclined chairs, back to back so that the headrests touched. Their leather covers were worn smooth with use. Aristide perched on one. Meanwhile, Raspail put on a headnet to call up a holographic display. She set it rotating in the vitrine. It was a mere jumble of lines, showing no structure at all. "This is a three-dimensional projection of the graph we will be working with," she said. "This is vastly simplified, of course. The display surface is actually folded through two other dimensions that cannot be shown, only experienced. Savants have spent whole careers inventing new topologies to vex us."

"What can you tell from a graph like that?" Dominique asked.

"From this? Nothing. It's pure trash. But what is disordered on one scale may show structure on another." She hit a key, and the display shrank to a point, bringing more of the image within view. After half a dozen displays had been reduced to spots on the screen, a ghostly regularity appeared. The tangles of disorder were embedded in a matrix of pattern.

"Everything depends on scale," Raspail said thoughtfully. "What makes no sense on one scale, may be the answer to everything on another."

She stood up, her face severe. "You have had your first lesson. Now go back and wait for us. We have work to do."

Disappointed, Dominique said, "Can't I just watch?"

"No," Raspail said. "This is between us." She put a hand possessively on Aristide's arm.

Dominique backed out the door.

☼

The empty apartment seemed very quiet. Dominique stood for a while at the window, staring across the snowy valley to the unscalable west wall of Mont Chatoyer. It seemed very distant from here. Just as his mind began wandering back to home, he noticed that the window frame was gouged, as if someone had tried to dig through it with a pocket knife.

He turned back into the living room. What he had taken for a library the night before was in fact a large collection of disks with a few real books mixed in, all full of pictures without a line of type. Behind a chair he found a well-worn DI helmet and put it on to try out some of the disks. Most were labeled only with dates, so he picked one at random.

As soon as he lowered the eyeshades, he found himself back in the control room, lying on one of the chairs, staring up at the domed ceiling. The resolution and detail were far better than any DI he had ever experienced. He could actually feel the leather, the weight of his body, the hum of machinery around him. Before he had a chance to take it all in, the recording went on.

A bubble appeared in the air above the bridge of his nose. He—or the person whose experience this disk recorded—closed his eyes, and the world was transformed.

He was floating in a crystalline landscape under a flowering fractal tree. Above him, colors he had never seen before shivered down the sky. He watched, entranced, till someone touched him, sending a cascade of sensation through his body. The feeling was intensely erotic.

He spun around, realizing in mid-motion that he no longer had a body; he was no more than an algorithm in phase space. And yet sensation was even more intense, as if flesh were a poor transmitter, and he now felt raw stimulation pouring unimpeded into his brain. A glittering stream of air caressed him, and he knew instinctively it was Raspail. The pulse of feeling that followed made the part of him that was still Dominique squirm in discomfort. Against his will he felt his body inflamed with a strange, abstract desire. Slowly she blended with him, merging, running through him like a stream. He was closer to her than it was possible for anyone to be; every nerve in her body kissed one of his. He felt a rush of erotic adoration that wasn't his own.

Guilty and overstimulated, he raised his hand to shut the helmet off. But as he moved the scene changed. Raspail withdrew from him, leaving him feeling small and empty, like half a person. Now he was surrounded by a crackling web of threads that flared and buzzed dangerously where they crossed. They were close to his naked nerves. Gingerly he reached out to deform the web. With a painful snap of electricity, one thread broke. Blood spurted from the severed end, drenching his face. As it hit him it began to crawl. It was a spray of maggots, wriggling, hungry for his brain. He wanted to scream, but they were all over his face, burrowing at his eyes, crawling into his ears and nose. He could feel them wriggling inside his eyeballs; they began to eat away at the scene before him, revealing another, darker scene beneath. A visceral terror gripped him; he didn't want to see the hidden thing they were revealing. Yet he was paralyzed, unable to stop looking.

There was a crash. Dominique ripped off the helmet and threw it across the room. He saw Aristide bolt through the door and into the kitchen, his face pasty white. Putting a hand out to steady himself, Dominique brought the rest of his mind back. He went to the kitchen door. Aristide was vomiting violently into the sink.

At length Aristide turned on the faucet and splashed cold water in his face. He turned, saw Dominique, and froze.

"What's wrong?" Dominique said. He felt a little queasy himself.

"Nothing," Aristide said tensely. "I'm fine. If Raspail asks, tell her that. Promise?"

Dominique was too confused to do anything but nod. Aristide drew himself up and started toward the bedroom, holding onto the wall. His eyes kept tracking to the left, as if trying to follow a room that was spinning around him. When he came to a halt, swaying, Dominique took his arm and began to lead him. Aristide clutched his shoulder in terror. "I'll fall," he said. "It's too far down."

"Don't worry, I'll catch you," Dominique said.

When they reached the bed, Aristide curled up on it in fetal position, eyes closed. Dominique hovered anxiously over him. "Can I get you something?" he asked.

Aristide's eyes snapped open, looking straight into Dominique's. "I'll break your brain across my knee if you try to take her," he whispered.

"I won't," Dominique said.

Aristide's eyes drifted leftward again, then closed. "You're a good one, Dominique. Don't tell Raspail."

The living room no longer seemed quite so comfortable. Dominique moved restlessly from chair to chair, avoiding the DI helmet that had landed on the couch. He tried to look at the picture books, but the images seemed disjointed and senseless.

Hours later, Raspail came back. Her step was light, and there was an elated, buoyant look to her. She held up a spool and said, "I've got it. This is the graph the savants have been waiting for." She tossed it across the room; Dominique scrambled to catch it before it hit the floor. Raspail had already turned toward the kitchen. When she came back with a drink in her hand, she went to the couch and picked up the helmet. Dominique realized he had left it running all this time.

"Did you try this?" she said, popping the disk out and glancing at it.

Dominique's neck grew uncomfortably hot; did she know what was on it? "I didn't think—" he stammered.

"I suppose it can't do you any harm, not like the real thing. We tried to record sessions in Oracle for a while, but it was useless. The resolution is too poor. It was not even close to vivid enough." She looked at him, frowning slightly. "Did you see anything?"

"Only a little," Dominique said, feeling sweaty. He could barely meet her eyes.

"Next time you should try the training simulations, over here. They hone the perceptual skills you will need as a voyant. You will have to get very good at all of them before I can let you try Oracle."

Dominique was no longer certain he wanted to try Oracle. He itched to tell her about Aristide, but he had given his word. "How long does it take? The training, I mean."

"It varies." Raspail waved a hand vaguely.

"Well, how long has Aristide been?"

Her face lost its openness. "He is a special case. He was an acolyte before I discovered him. It damaged him."

"Damaged?" Dominique said, eyes widening.

"He learned to read. I have had to unteach him. It has taken a long time. You will not have to worry about that."

Dominique was silent, thinking of the different story Aristide had told him. Why should either of them lie? He found himself staring at the spool Raspail had tossed to him so casually. "What is it you've discovered?" he said.

Stretching out her legs, Raspail chuckled. She didn't exactly look happy—Dominique was not sure that was possible—but she did look triumphant. "I don't know," she said. "The savants don't always tell us what the data signify. All I know is, it will be completely unexpected. It relates the algorithms in a way no one has ever imagined."

"Will they be able to predict the future now?"

She looked puzzled. "What makes you say that?"

"I thought you were studying the patterns of history."

"Oh, yes. But we have long since proved that prediction is impossible."

"Then what are you trying to find?"

"You are falling into the old deterministic fallacy, like scientists back in the days before the Renaissance Dernier." She rose and paced across to the window, where the setting sun cast shadows over the complex planes of her face. She looked like the statue of an enigma.

She said, "There was once a scientist named Laplace who imagined that we lived in a clockwork world. The universe, he thought, was a mechanism that would be perfectly predictable if only we knew the rules. For generations, people believed that everything was ultimately reducible to linear formulae. Respectable savants even said that history could be forecast, once we nailed down certain psychological variables.

"What they didn't know was that not even perfect clockwork, not even the motion of the planets, is predictable on a larger scale. Every natural process has an element of chaos in it, which makes it inherently unpredictable. It may not show itself on our scale, but it is there. Thank God. If we actually lived in a world like the one Laplace described, it would be impossible to generate new information. We would be locked in a perpetual order crisis—an eternal, perfect stasis.

"But that is not true. The universe is not deterministic; it is complex and stochastic. Information is continually being created, leading from uniformity to variety. Nature generates its own novelty. So the future is fundamentally different from the past. Looking backwards, we see less and less information. Ahead, there are novel new forms of complexity. We cannot predict them, because they are generated through random processes. It is that randomness we need to seek out. Disequilibrium is the creative state. It leads through confusion to a higher order of order."

Her low voice held a thrill of conviction. It gave Dominique an insecure feeling. "But—" he started.

"Yes?"

"Randomness can destroy, too. Don't you run a risk of losing the order we have?"

She stood still, looking out the window. Dominique watched the light fade on her face as the sun traveled beyond the mountain ridge. There was a deep crease between her eyebrows. She said, "Do you believe in evil, Dominique?"

It was not the answer he had expected. He stammered, "Well, I believe people sometimes do harmful things."

"No, I don't mean stupidity, or malice, or anything that can be avoided. I mean evil that is woven into the fabric of a situation so that there is no way of avoiding it. A terrible course that draws you in, and you can't stop and can't go back, so you just continue on, knowing that you are doing harm, and will do more before the end."

He said nothing. At last she turned to look at him. "That is a matter of scale, too. On the micro scale of human lives, randomness may cause harm. I have to be concerned with a larger scale."

That evening, Raspail's openness bled away, leaving the silent, moody person Dominique had seen before. They ate supper without exchanging a word, Raspail starting tensely at every sound. Through the whole evening she never asked about Aristide.

When Dominique came into the darkened bedroom that night, Aristide had not moved. Dominique silently lit a new candle in the window before going to bed. He slept uneasily under the dangling bottles.

🕯

The next morning when Dominique woke, the other bed was empty. When he came out into the living room he stopped in his tracks. The shelves had all been emptied, the disk boxes dumped in a pilfered heap on the floor. The disks filled the air, dangling on threads from the light fixtures, the curtain rods, the furniture. Their rainbow surfaces winked and flashed in the morning sun, a dazzling galaxy of round-eyed stars. Dominique threaded his way into the room, ducking to avoid tiny rotating suns. He wondered how they would ever get the disks back into the proper boxes.

Aristide was sitting like an allegorical god on the bottom of an overturned chair, wrapped in a sheet, his head surrounded with spinning disks. "Guess what, Dominique?" he cried out.

"What?"

"We have a day off. Raspail's gone down into the savants' den to throw them some red meat. We can do whatever we want. What do you want?"

Dominique said, "Whatever you usually do on a day off."

"Good! I'll take you to see the salle des cerveaux, then."
He jumped up as if to start off right then and there.

"You can't go like that," Dominique said.

Aristide looked down, saw that he was dressed only in
a sheet, and broke into laughter.

Half an hour later, Dominique was trying to keep up
with Aristide as he darted like a loose electron down the
hallways of Sorel. All of the previous day's malaise was
gone; Aristide acted like his veins were running with electricity. He kept Dominique laughing the whole way to the
east wing.

"Wait here," he said at one doorway. "Don't come in
till I call."

When Dominique heard the call, he stepped through.
The room before him was a large open cortile filled with
a maze of stairways he would have to thread, down then
up, to reach the spot where Aristide stood on the other
side. He took a step, but stopped, blinking. The stairways
were impossible ones—disconcerting trompes l'oeil that
made a mockery of dimension. One veered sideways, disappearing into a vertical wall painted so cleverly that the
steps seemed to continue on in two dimensions, though no
person could climb them. Another switchbacked so that
the only way to climb every other flight was upside-down.
Another passed through an archway then continued on,
tilted sideways. Dominique could see no path for anything but a two-dimensional image to get through.

Across the room, Aristide was laughing hysterically at
his reaction. "Here, Dominique!" he called. "Come on.
You can do it!"

Dominique stepped over a painted drop, then stopped,
seized with vertigo. His feet told him he stood on solid
ground, but his eyes told him otherwise. "I can't," he said.

Still laughing, Aristide ran lightly down a stairway,
jumped to another, then followed a winding path through

the maze till he stood at Dominique's side. "You really *are* a voyant," he said.

"What do you mean?"

"The savants are such numbskulls they can barely see the illusion, much less be confused by it."

"I thought the savants were really smart," Dominique said.

"Not in our way. But then, we're not smart in their way, either."

Dominique laughed. "I know I'm not."

Aristide took his arm. "Here, I'll show you across."

It took a nerve-racking half-minute of stepping over painted precipices. When he stood safely on the other side he blew out a breath, glad it was over. "Is that the salle des cerveaux?" he asked.

"Oh no, just a game," Aristide answered.

As they continued on they began to meet acolytes hurrying past, eyeshades studiously lowered, and clusters of saffron-robed savants holding discussions in the hallways. More than one conversation broke off as they passed.

"Why are they staring?" Dominique whispered to Aristide.

"It's an old tradition," Aristide answered breezily. "The east and west wings don't mix much. Savants think; voyants see. They think we're 'surface personalities.' We think they're pompous dopes."

They came to a monumental entryway that had once been on the exterior; later construction had swallowed it, making it look out of proportion. Aristide led the way through tall doors into a lobby. At a desk a tall, portly woman was staring disdainfully at their approach.

"What do you want?" she demanded.

"To marry you, Charron," Aristide said.

"Get out of my library."

"You'll break my heart."

She clenched her jaw as if to force back words she might regret. "I suppose you want to see the salle des cerveaux."

"Thank you."

"Wait while I get the key."

The librarian lumbered heavily off. Dominique was aware that several scholars were staring coldly at them. He could not fit Aristide's explanation to the acutely personal hostility he sensed. One savant—a handsome man with thick brown hair and a gray-shot beard over a strong chin—looked about to rise and confront them.

"You see him?" Aristide whispered. Dominique nodded. "That's Gaspard Desnoyer, the noetic architect. Watch out for him. He's tried to murder me."

Dominique stared at his companion, but Aristide's expression was as carefree as it had been all morning. "Are you serious?"

"Oh, yes. You see, he used to be Raspail's lover. Things went wrong, and now he is her enemy."

The librarian was beckoning at them from a doorway. When they reached her, she turned to lead the way down an aisle of study cubicles. Walking behind her, Aristide mimicked her rolling gait, making a pair of acolytes in a nearby cubicle explode in laughter. Charron whipped round, but Aristide was all innocence again.

They came to a double set of black lacquer doors with ornate silver fittings. The librarian waved her keycard before a lock panel, and the entry light flashed on. "The surveillance is on," she said. "Don't touch anything."

Dominique had intended to ask Aristide what he meant by "murder" as soon as they were alone, but at the remark about surveillance he put the question away for later.

The salle des cerveaux was empty, and very still. The walls were made of polished stone so black it disappeared in the dim light, giving the illusion of great space. Along the walls, on identical black pedestals, stood holo projections, each display floating in dark air.

Dominique approached the first projection. "It's a diatom graph," he said. His voice sounded loud in the silence.

"This is the savants' reference collection," Aristide whispered. "The graphs they study are preserved here. There are millions on file. But these aren't the ones I want you to see."

He led Dominique through a chain of dark rooms, all lined with minds from the past. There were athletes and musicians, statesmen, philosophers, and tyrants. One chain of rooms held pathologies: autism, paranoia, dementia. Dominique lingered before a species of psychosis, wondering how to tell it from the normal graphs.

"I thought these diseases didn't exist any more," he said.

"They don't," Aristide answered. "They're gone, just like criminal pathologies. Diatom graphs made it possible to cure them. Until we had a way of telling the diseases apart and measuring whether therapies did any good, no one knew what worked. It was just guesses. You wouldn't believe some of the things they did."

"Is everyone's diatom graph on file?"

"No, dataspace is too valuable. They just keep statistics and benchmarks. Come on, this way."

They came to a long, narrow gallery that curved out of sight before them. Here, there were no vitrines; the delicate webwork spheres had been sculpted in glass, some tinted, others silver. The only light was on the art works, making them glow as if from within.

Aristide pointed to the plaque on the first pedestal, which held only the name Bernaud. "The first Voyant of Sorel," he said. "This room has all the great ones."

"Why are they done in glass?" Dominique asked.

Aristide shrugged. "It's a tradition."

Dominique walked down the line of sculptures, dazzled by their crystalline clarity. It took several minutes for him to notice the common feature. On the interior, the glass strands followed a myriad of patterns; but on the outside surface all were the same.

"That is called the Bernaud pattern," Aristide explained. "A person must have it in order to interface with Oracle. It is the result of the training Raspail told you about."

"So these patterns aren't natural?" Dominique asked.

"What's natural?"

"Well, these aren't the diatom graphs they were born with?"

"No one has the graph they were born with. Graphs change all the time; that's what learning is. Of course, Oracle causes changes you can't learn any other way. They choose apprentices for their similarity to the Bernaud pattern. It makes the training go faster."

"How long have you been in training, Aristide?" Dominique asked.

Aristide was silent a moment, staring at the sculpture before him. "I don't know," he said at last.

It was a clumsy evasion, but Dominique decided to let it drop.

As they walked on down the line, Dominique noticed a change. The first sculpture had been simple and symmetrical, the glass strands linked in a self-repeating geometry. But farther down the gallery, the graphs became more tangled. They branched like elm roots before reaching the resolution of the outer surface.

"They think there has actually been a change in mental organization," Aristide said. "Diatom graphs like Bernaud's don't exist any more. Every generation it gets a little harder to find apprentices whose graphs are close enough. Always the training takes longer."

The last sculpture in line was Raspail's. It had an odd, mirror-image structure, full of patterns reversed upon themselves. Aristide gazed at it, entranced. "They installed hers just last year, when even the savants had to admit she was as great as Bernaud. It's the most beautiful graph here."

The gallery stretched on in darkness, waiting for more sculptures. Dominique nudged Aristide. "Is yours going to be here?"

"Raspail is making it herself," Aristide said, looking off to where it would stand, beside his teacher's.

"But you're not even a voyant yet," Dominique said, surprised.

"She knows what she is doing."

They walked back to the lacquer doors in silence.

When they reached the door of the library again, Gaspard Desnoyer was waiting for them. He fell in step beside Dominique. Aristide pretended not to see.

"Introduce me to your friend, Aristide," the savant said.

"Piss off, Gaspard," Aristide answered. "You're such a sore loser."

Gaspard turned to Dominique and offered his hand. "I'm Savant Desnoyer. I take it you are Raspail's new apprentice."

His handshake was vigorous; his face looked not at all homicidal. But then, Dominique was not stealing away his lover. "I'm Dominique Cadot," he said.

"I've seen your diatom graph. Very impressive. We're glad to have you here."

"Bite him, Dominique," Aristide said.

"Oh, we're full of wit today, aren't we?" Gaspard said acidly.

"I can't speak for you," said Aristide. "You don't seem to have enough wit to know when you're acting like an out-of-work gigolo."

Without a word, Gaspard gathered the front of Aristide's garment in his fist and lifted him briefly off the floor; Aristide dangled like a puppet, his face blank with surprise. Then Gaspard propelled him backward down the hall to a small doorway and waved a keycard before the lock panel. When the door sprang open on a maintenance closet, the savant thrust Aristide forcefully into it. Hoses and brooms clattered down as Gaspard slammed the door and keyed in a lock code. None of the other savants walking in the hall even paused.

Gaspard took Dominique's elbow in a firm grip and led him away down the hall. "Now we can talk sensibly, without that moron in the way."

Stunned, Dominique looked back at the closet door. There was not a sound from inside. "But—"

"Oh, don't worry about him," Gaspard said. "The idiot will find a way out. He always does." His voice dropped. "I want to talk to you alone. I think it's important you know the truth about what's going on here."

"How has it been going?" Gaspard asked.

"What?"

"The training."

They sat in an alcove in a lounge shaped like the inside of a lung. Groups in saffron robes and eyeshades occupied other booths, the spongy walls drinking the sound of their voices.

Uneasily, Dominique said, "She says I have to learn all sorts of training simulations before I can try Oracle. It'll take a long time."

"Don't believe her!" Gaspard said fiercely. He reached over and grasped Dominique's arm as if to infuse him with combativeness. "You can start on Oracle now, I know it. She's just stalling so her boytoy's incompetence won't become obvious. Don't let her do it. Demand your rights."

Dominique shifted uncomfortably. He didn't want to get caught up in this intensely personal war.

At Dominique's hesitation, Gaspard's eyes narrowed. "What has that liar told you about me?"

"Listen, I'm not on anyone's side," Dominique said.

"Not yet," Gaspard said.

"I'm not going to be."

"If you don't know both sides, you're on one of them through sheer ignorance. Do you know about me and Raspail?"

"Is it true?"

"Oh, yes. It was the old attraction of opposites, I suppose, the marriage of intellect and inspiration. I lived with her in the west wing for years. But it all started going bad seven years ago, when she discovered that 'apprentice' of hers. He was thirteen."

"Seven years?" Dominique said. At last he knew how long the training took.

Gaspard shifted as if something were pricking him. "It's become the Institut's nasty little secret. Even the maintenance staff have guessed by now that training is the least of what they're doing."

He frowned off over Dominique's shoulder, into the past. "I've known all along, in a way. There was nothing about his graph that suited him to be a voyant. I thought she would get bored with his adolescent infatuation, if I only waited. But Oracle is a land we can't imagine, and that's where they spent their time. She became obsessed. And I became irrelevant, and finally inconvenient."

His voice had turned bitter; he forced himself to shrug as if it meant nothing. But he still radiated anger like a stove coil hot enough to burn but not to glow. "She could have trained five voyants in the time she's wasted pretending to train him. When they started, we had three voyants who were barely keeping pace with the demand. Now the other two have retired or died, and everyone is still waiting for Aristide to take over part of the work. The truth that no one wants to believe is that he never will.

"Meanwhile, our research is at a standstill; savants have to wait in line six months for time on Oracle. The whole east wing is in a state of revolt. It's intolerable, especially at such a critical time. If Raspail weren't doing the best work of her career, no one would put up with it. But all I can think of is what she could be doing if he weren't wasting her time."

Gaspard's voice had risen again; he stopped himself. "Of course, my personal feelings don't enter into this. I am first to admit, Raspail is at the pinnacle of her career. The work she is doing is brilliant. She has to be freed, for the good of Sorel."

Dominique looked away, feeling as if just being here was participating in Gaspard's self-deception. When he looked back, the savant had an expression of eager hungriness. "That's where you come in. Your arrival was a godsend. She can't say you're unsuited; she *has* to train you. It may be the thing to break the impasse. A lot of hopes are riding on you."

Dominique felt like hiding under his chair. He didn't want this responsibility.

Gaspard glanced up and stiffened; Aristide was leaning casually against the entrance to their alcove.

"Finished feeding him poison yet, Gaspard?" Aristide asked. He had a new rip in one sleeve and a smudge of dirt across his forehead.

Gaspard pointedly turned back to Dominique. "I'd like to talk to you again soon, to hear about your progress."

Taking this as his cue, Dominique rose to go. "Sure. Thanks."

"Good luck," Gaspard said.

As the two apprentices walked back, Dominique could make new sense of the glances the savants cast their way. The contempt wasn't meant for him; it was all directed at Aristide. The voyant's toy. The dirty secret of Sorel.

"You didn't believe him, did you?" Aristide said in a low voice. He walked with a defiant posture.

"I don't know," Dominique said.

"I thought you were supposed to be loyal."

"If he was lying, then why won't Raspail let me see anything? Why is she shutting me out?"

In a barely audible voice, Aristide said, "She's afraid you'll find out too much."

Dominique hesitated, then said, "You mean about you and her? Why should I care how you spend your spare time?"

"That's not what I mean."

"Then what?"

"I'm not supposed to tell you."

And Dominique couldn't get another word out of him the rest of the way back.

When they arrived at the voyant's quarters, Raspail was waiting anxiously at the door. "Did you go to the east wing?" she asked Aristide.

"Yes," he said, passing by her into the apartment. She followed him closely, leaving Dominique to close the door.

"I wish you wouldn't do that," she said.

With a false lightness Aristide answered, "I just had to check whether they still hate us as much as ever. I shouldn't have bothered."

Raspail's voice was tight with tension. "Don't worry about them, Aristide. They will eat their words."

"Yes, but will I be around to see it?" He went into his room and closed the door.

Raspail stood staring after him, her whole body stiff, one hand clutching at her throat. When she turned round, her face looked stricken.

Dominique went into the kitchen and turned on the faucet so he couldn't hear another word. He opened a cupboard and began rummaging loudly for a bowl to make some salad in.

Was this how history was made? Were the crucial branching points ruled not by the great forces of cultural evolution but by personal jealousies and wars of thwarted love?

Great events were not supposed to be like this.

*

The sky outside the Rinpoche's chamber was the utter black of a lunar day. The rugged gray terrain of Mare Nectaris stretched to the sudden horizon. Overhead, the bright sickle of a crescent Earth hung motionless in the sky. Neither the Rinpoche's Voice nor Gaspard Desnoyer spared it a glance. They were both bent over the display in the holo vitrine.

It showed the graph of Barrère's data that Raspail had produced: an abstract sculpture of sharp, slashing lines and intermittent snow. "How can Raspail make sense of this?" Gaspard said. "I can't understand it, even abstracted and simplified like this."

"I find it unsettling," Naidu said.

"It damn well should be. It proves what trouble we're in if the Redpath phenomenon grows."

Naidu rubbed her temples. It had not been a good day. Something the Rinpoche had done—she was not even sure what—had set her off, and she had cried uncontrollably for two hours. It had left her with a splitting headache. But even the physical pain could not mask the underlying emptiness.

Gaspard was watching her. He had been analyzing her graph for ways to help her. He said, "You should think of getting back to your work, Naidu, instead of spending the days mourning him."

Getting back to her work meant letting someone else operate her. "I couldn't," she said. "It would seem like a desecration to let someone else in, where he once was."

"It's as if you've become imprinted on him," Gaspard said. "He should never have used you so exclusively. It just shows how dangerous this improved DI technology is. And the Redpaths want to give it to everyone."

With an effort, Naidu brought her mind back to the problem at hand—Savant Barrère's theory about the source of social imbalance. The spread of DI technology had the potential of a new communication revolution, but completely different from all the previous ones. All communication technology up to now—language, print, electronics—had excelled at transmitting rational, linear thought. The DI was useless at that, but had leaped ahead at transmission of perception, motor skills, and emotion. Widely used, it would foreground the instinctive, emotional side of the human psyche and devalue the rational.

"We may not be able to stop it," Naidu said. "It may not be our place to stop it."

"No one's arguing for stagnation," Gaspard said. "All we want is control. We outgrew rapid, uncontrolled change along with the other evils of pre-Renaissance society. We don't let our civilization run amok any more, charging randomly into success or catastrophe. We're not gypsy moths or viruses. We choose our future. That's what makes us human."

With a few keystrokes, Naidu brought up the graph showing the line of human culture threading over the rough landscape. She backed it up several centuries. Here, the culture line was not a single stream, but a myriad of rivulets spread over the wide boundary between stagnation and chaos. When they met an obstacle some of the lines went off the scale while others threaded around or through and survived to branch again. But as the simulation ran forward, the tangled skein of human cultures converged and interwove into a thick rope.

"That is our underlying problem," she said. "Our civilization has become too uniform. A millenium ago there were hundreds of languages, thousands of cultures, even more world views. Now, we are dangerously converged. The mindset of the Instituts is the norm for all. One truth is everyone's truth. It makes us less adaptable. In a way, we have brought this on ourselves."

"There are advantages to uniformity, or we wouldn't have gotten this way," Gaspard said. "Nowadays, no one kills anyone else who sees the truth a little differently."

"Advantages on the individual scale may not be advantages for the species."

"Yes, but how can we re-diversify?" Gaspard said. "Introduce ethnic conflict? Economic polarization? Nationalism? You've got a stronger stomach than I if you can do that." The light from the holo vitrine cast deep shadows on his face.

Naidu felt a longing for simpler times, when she only had to become the Rinpoche to find answers. Her job now was to think as the Rinpoche would have thought. She said, "Perhaps the Redpath phenomenon is our culture's own way of re-diversifying. A natural response to the danger. After all, they have begun by sowing distrust of the Instituts, which are the unifying forces of society."

"The Instituts steer the culture," Gaspard said. "Changes that affect us automatically propagate throughout society. If something creates widespread distrust of us, it could trigger an uncontrolled phase transition."

"You mean a random avalanche. Society could collapse."

"Or, if it can't adapt, cease to be." Gaspard shook his head tensely. "The slightest change in conditions could trigger it. Bad weather, or an unchecked rumor. Not to mention a troop of Redpath demagogues accusing us of secret conspiracies."

Naidu thought of her own simulations of the internal workings of Sorel and said, "Does Raspail know about this?"

Shaking his head, Gaspard said, "We have enough loose cannons without that."

Naidu looked out at the Earth hanging in the sky like a fragile glass ornament. "I wish we knew what we were doing," she said.

🕯

Breakfast the next morning was eaten in silence. Soon after, Raspail and Aristide disappeared into Oracle. This time, the voyant wouldn't even let Dominique past the door.

He spent some time trying out the training disks, but they quickly lost his interest. After ten minutes wandering aimlessly around the apartment, he decided to go down into Oracle, permission or no permission.

Descending the silent rampway, Dominique felt even more vividly the sense of some inconceivable intelligence, aware of him. It was in the still air, in the bland lighting, in the dustless floor. When, halfway down, he heard footsteps ahead, the back of his neck prickled with premonitions, and he darted into one of the empty doorways, listening.

The footsteps drew closer, but they did not sound like either Raspail's or Aristide's. They were halting, uneven. Dominique waited, trying to still his breath. The closer the steps came the slower they got, till Dominique could not stand waiting any longer and peered out.

It was Aristide after all, but walking drunkenly, veering from side to side, one foot dragging behind the other. When Dominique stepped out into the corridor he said in a slurred voice, "My rescue dog!" The pupil of one eye was dilated, the other normal. He put out a hand to touch the wall, but it was too far away, and he teetered. Dominique caught him before he fell.

They made their way together up a ramp that seemed to have turned endless. Aristide kept seeing imaginary precipices at his feet, and Dominique had to coax him across them. By the time they reached the apartment, Aristide had become too terrified to put one foot in front of the other. Dominique had to drag him the last few feet into bed.

It had begun to snow outside. Dominique sat on the edge of his cot, watching the random paths of the flakes in the blustery air, feeling trapped. Suddenly, Aristide sat bolt upright, staring tensely out the window.

"What are those?" he said, pointing.

"Snowflakes," Dominique said.

"No, they're not." All the color seemed drained from Aristide's face. He whispered, "They're maggots. They want to eat my brain."

He scrambled up and began clawing at the door. Dominique tried to coax him back to bed, talking soothingly.

"You'll never get her!" Aristide shrieked. "I'll kill you first!" He lunged for Dominique's eyes. Dominique tried to catch his wrists, but now Aristide was fighting ferociously. A vicious kick sent a stab of pain into Dominique's knee-cap, and before he could think, his fist went like a piston into the apprentice's stomach. Aristide gasped for breath and fell forward onto his knees, then to the floor.

Afraid that he had done some terrible damage, Dominique dragged the limp body to the bed then bent over, listening for breath. It was several seconds before Aristide gave a ragged gasp, then began breathing evenly. Heart pounding, Dominique settled back to watch.

Nothing happened for a long time. At last Dominique got up to go into the bathroom. His face had a bloody scratch, and there was some swelling in his knee. He went into the kitchen to get an ice pack but heard a sound from the bedroom and dashed back.

Aristide was standing wedged into a corner of the room, staring in terror around him. "Is it my blood?" he asked.

"Where?" Dominique said.

"On the walls, on the knives." Aristide grimaced in horror. "Oh my God, it's dripping from the ceiling." He tried to wipe something imaginary from his hair.

"Come on, back to bed. You'll feel better if you sleep."

"No!" Aristide pleaded. "It's all razors. Can't you see where it's cut me?" He held out a perfectly normal hand. "Look, the bone is showing."

"You're okay, there's no razors," Dominique said.

Step by painful step, he led Aristide across the room.

"Don't make me lie down in all that blood." Aristide was staring at his bed, shaking in terror. It made Dominique feel cruel, but he gently pushed Aristide down. His body stiff with revulsion, Aristide looked up into Dominique's face. For an instant, shifting clouds seemed to part, and out of his eyes looked a perfectly lucid person trapped in a malfunctioning mind.

"Something's gone wrong, hasn't it?" he said.

"Try to sleep," Dominique answered. "I'll be right here."

Raspail didn't come back till long after dark. When Dominique heard the hall door, he crept out quietly to talk to her. She was just disappearing into her bedroom when he called out, "Voyant!"

She turned back, one hand on the edge of her door. Her eyes were dark with exhaustion.

"Aristide's sick," Dominique said.

"I know," she answered calmly.

"No, you don't. He's crazy."

She nodded wearily. "It's just part of the training. Whenever he's immersed in Oracle for long, there is a reaction. It goes away. Don't worry about it." She stepped into her room and closed the door.

Dominique stood in the darkened living room, feeling abandoned. Don't worry about it? Easy for her to say.

He went back into the bedroom, grimly determined to stay on watch through the night. Once again he lit a fresh candle and settled crosslegged on his cot, eyes on Aristide.

Hours later, he was roused from sleep by a strange smell. He pulled himself erect to see Aristide sitting on the edge of his bed, face studiously intent as he held one hand over the candle flame. The smell was cooking flesh.

With a shout, Dominique seized Aristide's wrist. The entire palm was black and smoking. Swearing at himself, Dominique got up to get ice, salve, and bandages. Aristide watched carefully, silent, as he doctored the charred hand.

"Why did you do that?" Dominique demanded angrily, looking Aristide in the eyes. He looked calm and quiet.

"I couldn't feel my hand," Aristide said. "I thought maybe if I held it in the flame, I might feel it. I still can't."

"Well, you will in the morning."

"Why are you angry, Dominique?"

Dominique sighed. "I just don't want you to do that again."

"I won't."

Dominique sat back, vowing to stay awake this time.

By morning, Aristide was sleeping as if drugged. Feeling relieved of a terrible chore, Dominique stretched out his stiff limbs, then got up to go order some strong coffee. He was in the kitchen when he heard the peremptory rap on the hall door. He was coming out to answer it when Raspail came flying from her room and threw the door open. "Gaspard," she said, as if she had known exactly who it was going to be.

"I need to talk to you, Raspail," he said.

"What do we have left to talk about?"

"This is business. Institut business."

With a show of reluctance, she held the door open for him. There was an energy in the air between them, like that between electrodes. They went into the living room, and Dominique ducked back into the kitchen.

Their voices were low at first, and Dominique busied himself washing some dishes to avoid eavesdropping. But presently they began to lose their caution, and he could not avoid hearing.

"I'm trying to warn you, Raspail," Gaspard said. "The governing committee has lost patience."

"I don't show my work before it is done," Raspail said defensively.

Gaspard gave a low exclamation. "What are you trying to prove? Everyone already knows you're the best voyant alive. You're the only one who wants to hold you back, Raspail."

"We've been through this before."

"All right." He drew a breath. "I won't bring it all up again. The point is, Barrère's data has put the whole Institut in a turmoil. Everyone's clamoring for more studies. And for that, we need more than one voyant."

"You will have more than one. And it will be worth the wait."

"But when?"

"Soon."

"That's not good enough! Don't you know how urgent this is?"

Dominique heard the door to Aristide's room open. Quickly he stepped to the kitchen door to see what was going on. Aristide stood at the entrance to his room, swaying slightly. He looked more waiflike than ever, his eyes huge with shadows in a porcelain face. His attention was riveted on Gaspard.

Raspail was sitting on the couch, legs curled under her. Gaspard sat beside her, bent close. To Dominique's eyes, their body language screamed of the attraction between them.

When Aristide came forward, Gaspard rose.

"Savant Desnoyer," Aristide said. "It's been a long time."

Gaspard was watching him fixedly. "What's the matter, have you been ill?"

Aristide laughed a little giddily. "No. Just working hard to exceed the savants' expectations."

"What happened to your hand?"

Aristide looked down, as if perplexed to find his hand wrapped in bandages. It took a few moments of thought before he said uncertainly, "I...burned it." He looked to Dominique for confirmation. Dominique nodded silently.

Raspail said, "Aristide, Savant Desnoyer came to tell us that the governing committee wants a schedule for Dominique's training."

"Have you decided to make him your apprentice?" Aristide asked.

"That is not open to question," Gaspard answered.

"Two apprentices is a heavy load," Raspail said.

Aristide said brightly, "Don't worry. Another few months and he can be *my* apprentice."

Not if I have any say, thought Dominique.

"I'll be operating Oracle long before Dominique can start," Aristide went on. "He has a lot to learn."

Without warning, Gaspard reached out and grasped Aristide's wrist to look at his bandaged hand. Aristide wrenched savagely away. "Don't touch me! You're the one who put the knives in my bed, aren't you?"

Gaspard backed away, staring. "What are you talking about?"

"Get out!" Aristide shrieked. "Get out, before I set my dog on you."

Slowly, Gaspard said, "I'll see you later, Raspail."

When he was gone, Aristide turned anxiously to Raspail. She sat staring at the wall, looking too discouraged to move or speak.

"Let's get back to work," Aristide said.

She looked at him in disbelief. "Are you out of your mind?"

"We can't afford to rest," Aristide said urgently. "Didn't you hear? We have to work harder. I have to be ready."

She rose, her face dark with the presentiment of failure. "I am going down to Oracle. Alone."

When she was gone, Aristide sank into a chair. After a few moments of silence, he looked up at Dominique. "Do you think I won?"

"I don't know," Dominique said.

"He wants her back," said Aristide. "He can't have her. She loves me."

Not in the same way, Dominique thought. She loved Aristide all right, but not as a woman loves a man. And not as a mother loves a child, either. It was something else, something Dominique couldn't quite pinpoint.

"Will you be all right if I leave for a second?" Dominique asked.

Aristide looked as if it were the silliest question in the world. "Of course."

Two seconds later, Dominique was at the door to Oracle.

🕯

He found Raspail in the bottommost operating room, but she was not at the keyboard or in the operator's chair. She sat on a stool by the small glassblower's furnace, staring at the sculpture she had made, twisting its silk cover between her fingers.

"*Now* do you believe me?" Dominique said.

"I believed you before," she said.

She still didn't understand. He told her about last night. As she listened, shadows of despondence flickered across her face.

"We are so nearly done," she said, looking at the sculpture. "Yet every change gets harder. We may be against the limit to the elasticity of the mind."

She reached out and ran a finger down one branch of the glass diatom structure. The exquisite tenderness in her gesture brought a realization to Dominique. It was *this* she loved. This sculpture, this pattern. Not the person it symbolized.

"Is that Aristide's?" he asked.

"Not yet," she said. "Almost."

She went to the holo vitrine and put on the headnet. The display lit up with a diatom graph that looked like the pattern for the sculpture, or vice versa. A few small strands flashed red. "Those are the only ones still to go," she said.

It was a strange-looking graph, with none of the symmetry Dominique had seen in the sculptures of the salle des cerveaux. Its core was tangled, angular, rebelling against limits. Gradually, toward the outside, the jutting structure was disciplined into a thin veneer of Bernaud pattern. The graph had a weird, unsettling beauty. It reminded Dominique of something he couldn't quite place.

"It is in randomness that creativity lies," Raspail said. "Nothing new will ever exist without it. To make chaos is the most difficult, and the most profoundly creative, act a human can perform."

Her eyes on the glass sculpture burned with the afterglow of inspiration. "We must learn to imagine what has never been imagined before. To think anew."

It came to Dominique then what the graph reminded him of. And with that, a pattern fell into place.

He left Raspail still staring at her sculpture and climbed the ramp. Halfway up, he felt behind his ear for the chip the Rinpoche's Voice had given him. He pressed his thumb against it to send the signal.

He understood now what was going on. The savants hadn't seen the pattern because the crucial data was folded into the obscure dimension of the human heart.

Chapter 3

When Dominique reached the hallway, he decided not to go back to the apartment. Instead, he turned the other way and soon found himself exploring Sorel.

Right, then left, then right again—he hoped he would remember the way back, but didn't slow down. A door took his interest and he opened it—then stopped in confusion, for he was in the same distorted room where he had met the Rinpoche's Voice when he first arrived at Sorel. And there she was, waiting for him.

"Thank you for coming, Dominique," she said. He realized then that his trek through the building had not been his own choice, but carefully guided. He had just been operated by someone else, so subtly he had not even noticed. Automatically, his finger rose to the chip behind his ear. So it was more than just a communication device—it was an incredibly small DI link. He decided to get rid of it as soon as he could.

"What is it that made you wish to speak with me?" the Rinpoche's Voice said.

"I was down in Oracle's control room," he began.

"Yes," she said, in a tone so unsurprised that it struck him she could have been watching through his eyes. Everything he had done, everything he had seen, could have been observed. This time he had to restrain himself from reaching up and peeling the chip away.

"I saw Aristide's diatom graph," he said.

"Yes," she said again. A statement. So she *had* been watching, or recording it all without his permission. The thought outraged him. No wonder everyone in this place spoke in acrostics, never knowing when they might be overheard. Well, so would he.

"Riddle it out yourself," he said. "I've given you the clue. If you're so wise it shouldn't be hard."

He turned and left then, on his own volition this time.

When Raspail read the summons later that day, her face had a look of quiet desperation. She closed her eyes and drew a long, uneven breath before telling Dominique and Aristide that they had all been ordered to a meeting with the Rinpoche.

Dominique had not expected the Rinpoche's response to be so impersonal, or so threatening. He watched Raspail disappear into her bedroom to wait for the appointed time and felt like a secret traitor.

Aristide was huddled in the window seat. Dominique settled down beside him and followed his gaze out across the wintry valley to where a storm cloud was blundering its way toward the west face of Mont Chatoyer.

"I've seen that a thousand times," Aristide said. "The clouds are always smashing into the mountain, but the mountain always wins."

"Why is she so worried about this?" Dominique said.

"They're going to find out what we are doing," Aristide said.

"Is that such a bad thing?"

"They'll try to stop us. They don't *want* a phase transition, Dominique. It's too risky. At least the order crisis is safe."

"There's something I don't understand," Dominique said. "What do you get out of this, Aristide?"

Aristide looked as if the question were insane. "I get to be the most important person in Raspail's life."

Hesitantly, Dominique said, "I'm not trying to pry, Aristide, but do you think she really loves you?" Just make him think, make him question: that was all Dominique wanted.

"I *know* it," Aristide said, his eyes intense. "You've never been in Oracle; how could you know? There, we become each other. I've been inside her, all the way. I've seen through her eyes, thought through her brain. We're interwoven till there is no me or her, just a single stream of both of us."

"Is that healthy?" Dominique said.

"I don't care. If it's not, I don't want to be healthy."

When he saw Dominique's unsettled expression, Aristide said, "I could show you, Dominique. If you would just link up with me, I could take you into Oracle with us, and then you would understand."

Shifting uncomfortably, Dominique rubbed behind his ear where the chip was still fixed to his skin. He had been unable to get it off. It was reminding him that he had had quite enough of being controlled. "I don't like mind sharing," he said.

"Then you've never had a really skillful operator. It can be good. It can be unbelievable." Aristide's voice trailed away as his mind strayed. "But maybe some people just aren't suited for it. That was what broke up Raspail and Gaspard, you know. They tried to merge in Oracle and found out more than they wanted to know about each other. Their relationship was built on illusion and couldn't survive real intimacy. Ours isn't."

Dominique watched him, thinking that the ultimate mystery of Sorel lay inside Aristide's mind. It was a place he had no intention of going, ever again.

🕯

The Rinpoche's chambers lay at the very summit of Sorel. The three visitors climbed a helical staircase that started in a wide, gracious sweep around a central courtyard but wound tighter with every flight, like a spring increasing in tension. By the end they went in a dizzy single file with only a metal pole at the center of the spiral. Dominique was sure they had climbed long enough to pierce the top of Sorel's tallest tower and into the sky.

In fact, the Rinpoche's room seemed to be situated in the sky; from the large windows Dominique could see beyond the Vaudry Range to Neige Valley and the mouth of the Rive-Argent. Then the view moved, as if the room were turning in the wind, and Dominique looked away to avoid vertigo. The chamber was furnished with ascetic simplicity: a mat over a bare stone floor, a washstand, and a terminal with holo vitrine displaying a changing mandala. On pillows at one end of the room sat a group of people in saffron dhouras.

As Raspail approached, the savants rose in respect from their pillows. Raspail exchanged guarded nods with them. One was an elderly, sharp-faced woman with uncombed gray hair falling around her shoulders; another was a bald, round-faced Buddha of a man. The third was Gaspard.

The Rinpoche's Voice was there as well; Dominique was almost certain that she was being operated this time, since her face had the seamless, serene quality of an ancient statue. In a light, untroubled voice she said, "Welcome, Voyant Raspail. I have invited Savants Barrère,

Lalande, and Desnoyer to join our discussion because Oracle is so critical to their work."

They all settled down on pillows again. At a nod from the Rinpoche's Voice, Gaspard opened the meeting without any preliminary pleasantries.

"We all know what a critical time this is. Raspail's analysis of Barrère's data has proved that a phase transition is imminent. In order to act, we need information: and to get information we need Oracle operating at full capacity again."

Dominique glanced around at all the faces. This was not what he had expected.

Raspail sat with her back absolutely straight, her expression remote. "I will do all I can to cooperate," she said. "I can go to two shifts."

She already looked haggard. Gaspard said, more gently than before, "That's not the answer, Raspail. The answer is to have more voyants."

"You will have another, very soon," Raspail said.

There was a silence. "We will if you cooperate," Gaspard said at last. "Savants Lalande and Barrère have not yet seen the extraordinary opportunity that has come our way." He rose then, and went to the keyboard that controlled the holo vitrine. "Savants, this is the diatom graph of Dominique Cadot."

There was a stir of intaken breath when the vitrine lit up. Dominique leaned forward, understanding now what they saw, what he had not known the first time. The graph was an almost perfect Bernaud diagram.

"I don't believe it," Lalande said. "They are supposed to be extinct in nature."

"Obviously not," Gaspard said. "What most voyants need years of training to achieve, Dominique has as a gift. This graph is the most perfectly adapted to Oracle that I have ever seen."

They all turned to look at him. Dominique felt himself going red. He glanced at Raspail. Her face looked frozen.

The Rinpoche's Voice said, "How has he worked out, Raspail? Is his performance as good as his graph?"

"I have not had time to test him," she said stiffly. "I have been too busy."

Silence settled in again, colder than before. Raspail said defensively, "Aristide's training is at a critical phase. I could not drop it just like that."

The older woman, Barrère, broke in, "You have been using that excuse for four years, Raspail. I think I speak for most of the east wing when I say, our patience is used up. Now you have a real candidate, a candidate you can't fail with. The time has come for Aristide to graduate, or leave. He is holding you back."

They didn't understand. Dominique shifted on his cushion. Why couldn't they see the pattern?

"He will graduate, very soon," Raspail said. "He is almost ready."

"What does 'almost ready' mean? Show us his graph."

Raspail stiffened, and Aristide glanced at her apprehensively.

"I have not shown my design before," Raspail said. "I thought you would find it...unexpected. Surprising."

"What do you mean, 'your design?'" Gaspard said.

Reluctantly, Raspail rose and went to the holo vitrine. At the touch of her fingers, Dominique's simple, symmetrical graph faded, and Aristide's exploded into being, straining at its bounds, wrestling with itself. The savants leaned forward, drawn and repulsed by it. Raspail watched their reaction closely, a defiant smile growing on her face.

"I wouldn't call it beautiful," Barrère said, fascinated.

"A departure from tradition," the Rinpoche's Voice said, looking at the savants. "But what is wrong with that?"

"You asked how close we are to completion," Raspail said. "I will show you." She superimposed another graph on the screen. There was very little difference.

Barrère and Lalande gave exclamations of surprise. Raspail looked elated. But Gaspard was frowning, his hand stroking his beard fast.

"Except that is not Aristide's graph," he said.

Raspail's face iced over again.

"I have seen Aristide's graph," Gaspard went on. "I can't remember the details, but this is not it. I don't know what this is; it scarcely looks human. I'll show you the closest thing to it." He went to the holo and split the display, calling up a second image for comparison. It was a graph Dominique had seen in the salle des cerveaux. "Type Q psychosis," Gaspard said. "The textbook model."

There was no denying the resemblance. Dominique felt Aristide tense at his side, like an animal preparing to flee.

Unexpectedly, Raspail laughed. "You're not telling us anything we didn't know, Gaspard," she said. "Aristide and I knew we were treading on the edge of danger. It made the work exceedingly delicate. But the rewards are overwhelming."

Gaspard was frowning in perplexity. "Then this *is* his graph?"

"It is."

"Show me his original graph again."

"It's not relevant," Raspail snapped.

"I confess," said the Rinpoche's Voice calmly, "I also would like to see it."

Raspail looked as if the walls were lurching closer around her. She turned to the keyboard, and her fingers pounded furiously. The display dissolved and was replaced.

"My God," Gaspard said.

There was no resemblance at first glance. It was an ordinary graph, with none of the jarring beauty of the other.

The room was quiet. Only the Rinpoche's Voice looked unperturbed. "Raspail," she said, "how many alterations have you made?"

She swept them with an unapologetic gaze. "Five hundred and seventy-two."

Their faces looked frozen.

Raspail touched the keyboard and the display sprang to life, showing the sequence of changes she had made. It was like a chain reaction, starting at the center and working out. The image twinkled, collapsed, and was reborn from within. The savants watched, mesmerized, until the ordinary graph had been transformed into Raspail's design.

Gaspard looked shaken. "This is not training," he said. "You have made a new person."

"Yes," she said. "A person unlike any that has ever lived."

The Rinpoche's Voice looked at Aristide. "Is Raspail right? Five hundred and seventy-two?"

"I wasn't counting," Aristide said.

"Did you consent to this?"

"Of course," he said. "Before, I was just an ordinary person. She has made me more. Her design is inspired, a masterpiece. I would do it all again."

"We can't accept that testimony," Gaspard burst out. "This is scarcely a person any more. Every reaction in him has been created to serve Raspail's purposes. Do you think she would have left him any will to object? It would have jeopardized her scheme."

"That's not true!" Raspail strafed him with a look.

Gaspard's voice was steely. "This is a ghastly experiment. No human being has the right to alter another one this way. We have to stop it now."

"You can't do that," Raspail said, stepping instinctively closer to the holo vitrine, as if to protect the image in it.

"How can you defend this?" Gaspard said. "We all know what it takes to make alterations this severe." He looked at Aristide, then away, as if the sight were too horrible. "God, to think I used to be afraid you were lovers! I only wish now it were that simple. Seven years... What exactly is he to you, Raspail? Your slave? Your victim?"

"He is my art work," she said softly.

Aristide gave a wild laugh. "You've lost, Gaspard! Just admit it, why don't you? We've shared things you can't even imagine."

There was a reckless look in Raspail's eyes that was at least partly vengeful. "Yes," she said to Gaspard, "Through him, I have seen things no one else could. His sensations are acute enough to take your breath away."

Grimly, Gaspard said, "You have mind shared, then."

"You can't imagine how exhilarating it was," she said with a smile like cyanide.

"To go into madness and come out again unharmed, you mean?" Gaspard said.

"To be in a mind completely compatible with mine."

"You made it that way. You couldn't love a genuine person, so you had to create one."

"You're just jealous, Gaspard," Aristide broke in. "You've never had anyone inhabit you the way she's inhabited me." He looked around at the other savants with amused disdain. "And the rest of you. I bet you think it's funny to make your eyes float up like that. Well, balloons don't scare me any more. My needles can shine brighter than you can see."

Dominique caught his arm. "Shut up, Aristide!" he hissed.

Aristide froze, as if realizing he had made a terrible mistake.

The top of Savant Lalande's bald head was sprouting sweat. "This is an abomination," he said.

Gaspard had recovered control of his voice. Quietly, he said, "The only humane thing is to try and repair some of the damage Raspail has done."

"You're not going to touch him," Raspail said fiercely.

"For God's sake, Raspail!" Gaspard said. "Do you know what the world would think of this? If they knew we were abusing the technology like this, the Instituts would be pariahs. It would confirm all the Redpaths' worst accusations."

"You want to prevent bad publicity," she said bitterly.

"I want to prevent a great deal more than that," he said. "If the Redpaths could prove a piece of information like this, they could trigger events that would destroy our civilization."

Raspail didn't look as shaken as the others did. There was a craftiness in her voice as she said, "Then don't let the Redpaths know. Let me continue with my plan. As I said, his training is almost done."

"Make him a voyant?" Lalande said incredulously.

"You must be joking," Gaspard said. "We can't let Aristide operate Oracle. This graph is completely incompatible with it. The risk is appalling."

Dominique watched Raspail, expecting her to speak, but though her jaw worked she still said nothing. Unable to stand it, Dominique blurted out, "You don't understand, do you? He *has* been operating Oracle. For years now. Where do you think your great discoveries have been coming from?"

The savants turned to Raspail. She gazed over all their heads, ominous as a chained thundercloud.

"You said they were your discoveries, Raspail," Barrère said.

"I brought them back from chaos," she replied, as if speaking in a dream. "It's true, the graph is incompatible. I made it that way. Oracle fights him every moment he is in it. It has come seconds from destroying him. But it is from that conflict his insights arise. If he were suited to it, he would see only what we do. As it is, his mind is like lightning, illuminating in flashes. Sometimes the light shows nothing. Sometimes it shows everything."

She looked down then, focusing on them. "Yes, he's operated Oracle. He's been farther into it than anyone before him. Aristide is not trapped in our narrow confines of thinking. While we cling to the anchors of our security, he sails free, imagining things that have never been imagined before. He can already work in seven spatial dimensions, and three of time. He can see across the border into the next realm of reality. He is the one who will lead us into the phase transition. He will perceive a new world into being."

Her voice turned bitter. "But all you care about is your narrow ideas of sanity and good taste. Why do I bother? You don't want to see new worlds."

She turned, as if no one else were in the room, and went to the door. When Aristide saw she was leaving, he sprang up to follow her. Dominique hesitated a moment, glancing back at the stiff faces of the savants, then followed.

🕯

"I'm sorry," Dominique panted when they reached the bottom of the staircase. "I didn't know it would turn out like that. I didn't know they would—"

"It's not your fault," Raspail said. "This has been inevitable since we began." She put a hand on Aristide's shoulder and looked into his face. Dominique recognized that look now: it was the love of an artist for her work.

"They will try to mutilate you," she said to Aristide. "They will try to undo what I have done, to hide the evidence and calm their consciences."

80

"I won't let them," Aristide said.

"They can make you want it."

"No, they can't. I only want what you want. They'd have to take me apart to change that."

Raspail's shoulders hunched under some invisible weight. "They couldn't take you apart more than I have done already," she whispered. Then she turned urgently to Dominique. "You have to help us, Dominique. The savants will come after him as soon as they talk it out. Get Aristide out of here, away from Sorel. You know the world outside. You can find a place where he'll be safe, can't you?"

"I guess so…" Dominique stammered.

She turned to Aristide. "Go with him. Get away from here. You are precious to me, Aristide. I have to know you are safe."

Aristide didn't move. Raspail pushed him toward Dominique. "Go on, go with Dominique. Get away from us all. Go. Live."

"Come on, Aristide," Dominique said, taking his arm. This time, his instincts and Raspail's agreed. The best thing to do was to get away.

Aristide followed him like an automaton. Dominique hurried in the direction he thought the exit lay. They passed through a room whose floor circled like water going down a drain, then down a hall. There was a doorway at the other end; Dominique burst through it into sunlight. The snow was melting from the courtyard. All the gutters were atrickle, and bright rivulets ran across the paving bricks. The sky was brushed with clouds like wings. "Come on!" he yelled, giving a flying leap of exhilaration.

Aristide stood in the doorway, blinking through his hair like some nocturnal creature thrust under surgical lights. He peered out into the mountain air, then drew back again.

"What's the matter?" Dominique said, glancing around. It wouldn't be long before the savants discovered their whereabouts.

"I can't," Aristide said. He tried to take a step into the sunlight but jerked back, shaking. He braced himself, hands on the doorjambs. "It's too big out there," he said.

Dominique forced back his impatience. "There's nothing dangerous out here, Aristide. Back there is where the danger is. Let's go."

Visibly steeling himself, Aristide took three steps out into the courtyard.

As Dominique turned to lead the way, a wave of terror smashed down on him. He crouched like an animal on the pavement. The sky yawned above him, a huge, devouring cavity. He felt small, microbe-small, dwarfed by every brick and raindrop. Desperately, he looked around for something human-scale, and saw the door. Safety. He dashed toward it.

"Dominique?" Aristide knelt beside him as he cowered in the doorway, panting. He felt odd, unlike himself.

"I can't do it," he said. The words sounded distant. His heart was racing, and his skin tingled with aftershocks of fear.

"They've got you, too," Aristide said. "Of course. They want you, and your damned perfect graph. They're not going to let you go."

Dominique's hand rose to his ear, where the chip rested against his skull. He tried again to peel it off, but couldn't even get a fingernail under the corner.

Anger replaced the fear. They were controlling him, making him into something he wasn't meant to be, just like Aristide.

He fished out his pocket knife and put the blade behind his ear. Gritting his teeth, he sliced away a flap of skin, the chip still attached. He threw the bloody thing to the pavement and ground it into a puddle with his heel. A warm trickle ran down his neck. He swore, grimacing.

"Let's go," he said.

☀

The snow had melted from the roadways, and the village of Sous-Sorel was alive again. Dominique hadn't realized how accustomed he had become to seeing people masked in eyephones till he noticed that no one on the streets wore them.

He had half expected to be met by someone ready to take them back up the mountain, but there was no sign of any alarm or pursuit. He wondered if, despite its many powers, Sorel was like any other academic institution, better able to debate what to do than to actually do it.

At the hotel they learned that the bus wasn't coming for an hour. Dominique used the public booth in the lobby to place a call home for money. He recorded the message and chose a time-delay transmission. He didn't want to have to answer his mother's questions.

While waiting for the fund transfer, Dominique went into the bathroom to mop the blood off his neck and bandage the throbbing cut. When he came out he found Aristide staring out the window at the street, mesmerized. He looked like he scarcely believed what he was seeing.

"Has it been a long time since you've been outside Sorel?" Dominique asked.

"I've never been outside Sorel," Aristide said.

Of course. The person who had been outside Sorel was someone else.

"So what do you think of it?" Dominique said.

"It's so elaborate. I can't figure out why they spent the time to create all this. What kind of data structure does it symbolize?"

He thought it was an elaborate synthetic experience. "This is real, Aristide," Dominique said.

"How can you tell?"

"Well…I just can."

"But it looks like it's all built up from equations. Pretty simple ones, too."

"I guess it must be."

The clerk was watching them. It made Dominique nervous, so he took Aristide's arm and led him outside. As they walked down the street, Aristide kept stopping to stare at sights like a dog, a door handle, and a hanging sign.

They passed the bookstore. Looking in the window, Dominique saw a man in eyephones come out from the back room with an armload of books. When he flipped up the shades, Dominique realized it was Gabriel.

"So? I've got a job here," Gabriel said a little testily when Dominique came in, Aristide trailing behind. "Is that such an amazing thing?"

"No. Are you staying, then?"

"Why not? I can read everything the savants can read, and down here I can keep an open mind about it."

He had that "it was all my choice" tone he habitually used to elevate every setback into an ideological triumph. It had always driven Dominique crazy.

"Did they decide they didn't want you after all?" Gabriel said, stacking books.

Hesitating slightly, Dominique said, "Yeah. It wasn't a good match."

Aristide said at his side, "How can you be sure it doesn't represent a problem we're supposed to solve?"

He meant reality. "Maybe it does, Aristide," Dominique said. "Maybe it represents a whole lot of them." He explained to Gabriel, "This is Aristide. I met him up at Sorel."

"Hello," Aristide said.

"Are you an acolyte?" Gabriel asked, poised to be offended at any sign of condescension.

"No, I'm a voyant. The savants kicked me out because they thought I might start a phase transition."

Dominique stepped on his foot. But Gabriel hadn't heard; his attention was on something outside. "What are the Institut guards doing down here?" he said.

Dominique pushed Aristide down behind a book rack, then crouched out of sight, motioning at Gabriel, who was staring. "Look normal," he hissed.

Gabriel's eyes followed something outside; then he joined them behind the book rack, frowning. "What's going on?" he said. "Is it you they're looking for?"

"Gabe, do you have a back room or some place where we could stay out of sight, just till the bus comes?"

"You really *are* in trouble," Gabriel said wonderingly. "Don't worry, Nika. We can help you. I've got to tell Derosier." He headed for the back room. Dominique peered over the top of the book rack. There was a vehicle parked down the street with two people in gray dhouras by it. They didn't seem to be looking this way.

He wondered if he was overreacting. There was such a thing as the law. Sorel couldn't exactly kidnap two unwilling people in front of the whole town.

Or could they?

He looked at Aristide, trying to feel confident. "Once we're home in the Neige Valley, everything will be okay." He tried to imagine Raspail's exotic creation amid his down-to-earth family. His mother would never let him forget bringing home this particular stray.

Gabriel was gesturing from the back room. Crouched over to keep out of sight, Dominique and Aristide made their way to him. The back room was a wilderness of photonic equipment, some of it more advanced than even Dominique's mother had in her shop. The bookseller was there, eyephones pushed up on his forehead, looking suspicious.

"Just what I needed, two delinquents leading the savants right to my door," he said. "What did you do, steal office supplies?"

"They wouldn't send guards to hunt down pencils, Derosier," Gabriel said. "That one's the voyant." There was a hard edge to his voice that Dominique had never heard before. Like disappointment crystallized into a purpose.

The bookseller eyed Aristide. "Why are they after you?"

"Don't answer," Dominique said.

That seemed to be answer enough. "Just think, Derosier," Gabriel said. "A voyant would know how to access Oracle. We could get into the heart of their system."

"You don't want that, Gabe," Dominique said. "Believe me. It's dangerous. It's evil, what you can do with their technology."

"No technology is intrinsically evil," Gabriel said.

"Oh, give it a rest," the bookseller said. Then, to Dominique, "I'll see if we can help you." He pushed down his eyephones.

Gabriel had shifted position so he was blocking the door. He looked like a stranger. Dominique said, "I can handle this, Gabriel. We just need to get to the bus."

"The bus? With all the power of Sorel after you, you think you can get away on a bus?" He laughed. "Believe me, you need our help."

I don't want your help, Dominique thought. He looked around the crowded room for another door. There was only a small window, high on the wall.

Derosier flipped up his eyeshades and looked fixedly at Aristide. "Got that?" he said to the ether; Dominique realized he'd been transmitting the image. Now every Redpath on the net would know Aristide by sight.

The bookseller's expression had changed. "There's a vehicle on the way," he said. "It seems there has been unusual activity at Sorel for the past hour. I'm always the last to know."

"We don't need a vehicle," Dominique said.

"I think you do," Derosier answered. "Where did you think you were going to hide from them? We've got safe places."

The Neige Valley was seeming farther and farther away.

Derosier was distracted by another call on his head-net; he flipped down his eyeshades. At the same time they heard the front door open out in the shop, and voices.

"Hide," Gabriel whispered to Dominique. "I'll stall them." He slipped out into the shop.

Dominique headed for the window. It unfastened with a simple latch. He glanced back; Derosier was still distracted behind his eyephones. "Here, I'll boost you up," Dominique whispered to Aristide. "Meet me at the hotel. Don't let the guards see you." He cupped his hands for Aristide's foot, then lifted him up till he could slither through the narrow window.

Footsteps approached. Dominique dived behind a shelf unit crammed with old imagers.

"Sacré!" a man's voice said. "Look at all this equipment. Do you have a license for this stuff?"

"License, my ass," Derosier retorted. "I don't need a license." A heated, legalistic argument ensued. In the end, if the man had ever intended to search the room, he was thoroughly distracted.

Gabriel peered around the edge of the shelving. "It's safe now," he said. "Derosier's still yelling at him out on the street. Where's your friend?"

"He had to go," Dominique said.

Looking around, Gabriel spied the unlatched window. "Dominique, you idiot!" he cried out. "You ruin everything!" He hurried out to fetch Derosier.

Dominique dragged a table under the window and climbed up on it. It was a tighter squeeze for him than for Aristide; for a moment he thought he would get stuck. The Institut guards would have to pry him out. He gave a button-popping wrench and was through.

He landed in a mound of slush in a graveled alley. A dog barked at him from the fenced yard across the way. He looked both ways down the alley. The only sign of life was a man piling crates of produce into a truck down the block. Dominique headed toward the hotel.

As he was nearing the rear service entrance, a landcar came speeding down the alley, throwing off spray. It skidded to a stop beside him, and a man leaned out, his headnet covered with a beret. "Where's the voyant?" he said.

"I don't know. I'm looking for him," Dominique answered, one hand on the door latch.

"Bring him out here. I'll wait."

There was no one in the hotel lobby. When the receptionist saw him, she said, "There are some Institut guards looking for you."

"Thanks, I know. Have you seen my friend?"

She pointed to the street outside. Through the window, Dominique saw the guards ushering Aristide into a vehicle. They closed the door and seemed about to take off. At the same moment, the bus pulled up, its brakes hissing. Freedom on four wheels. If he just waited for the guards to leave, chances were good that he could sneak onto it and be miles away before anyone realized.

And then Aristide would be alone, facing whatever awaited him up at Sorel.

Dominique hesitated, poised on the edge of choice. Common sense told him there was nothing more he could do. He had failed to save Aristide; was it not best now to save himself?

It was no use; he felt responsible for Aristide. Squaring his shoulders, he pushed the door open and walked out onto the street. The guards spotted him at once, and the driver reported, "We've got the other one."

Dominique looked up at the jagged Institut buildings, wondering if he was doing the right thing. As if in answer, the wound behind his ear began to smart.

The driver steered uphill onto a lane that led to a broad loading dock built into the side of the mountain. The massive gray doors lifted and they drove through. Inside, the loading dock was cavernous and empty; the slamming of the car doors echoed hollowly. Three more guards were waiting. The leader gestured Dominique and Aristide to follow, and the other two fell in behind.

They were in a corridor, passing a nondescript door, when suddenly the lights went out, plunging them into complete darkness. In the confusion, Dominique felt Aristide grasp his wrist hard and pull him to the right, through the doorway. He followed blindly, turning several corners, moving fast. Aristide was back in his own reality now and perfectly confident of where he was going.

When the lights came on again no more than thirty seconds later, they were in a mazelike tangle of passages. "Where are we?" Dominique said.

"It's called the rootnet. That must have been Raspail, helping us. She knew those guards wouldn't be able to track me through here."

He headed for the west wing, with Dominique close behind. Back down the hallway of a thousand doors they raced. Aristide wrenched open the dust-seal doors and plunged down the curving ramp into Oracle's brain.

When they burst into the control room, Raspail was standing by the glass sculpture. She saw Aristide, and her face lit up with joy and desperation. She didn't embrace him; she held him at arm's length, her eyes feasting on his presence. She had the look of a relapsed addict.

"I should have known they would never let you get away," she said. "They don't want the evidence to leak out."

With a single finger, she touched Aristide's face. "You've always said yes to whatever I wanted to do. Will you say yes one more time?"

Aristide's eyes strayed to the operator's couch, then back to Raspail's face. Dominique said, "You don't have to agree, Aristide. You're free to say no."

Raspail's eyes never wavered from her creation. "In Oracle, you'll be safe. Once you are installed in the machine, they can't touch you. The phase transition will go on."

"Think, Aristide," Dominique said. "She doesn't love you; she loves having created you."

"Get out of here," Raspail snapped at him. "You've been their tool from the start."

"Just a second," Dominique said hotly. "I never pulled apart anyone's mind and put it back together all wrong."

"Don't blame Dominique," Aristide said earnestly. "He's only a dog."

Dominique took Aristide's arm. "Come on, Aristide. We'll come back later."

Angrily, Aristide shook off Dominique's hand. "You don't get it, Dominique," he said. "I don't want to be me. I want to be the person she loves."

He clasped hands with Raspail, as if to arm wrestle.

"Go away now, Dominique," she said softly. "Leave us be."

His first impulse was to obey, to back off and leave them. But as soon as he had passed through the door he stopped, mistrusting his own judgment. Nothing they did was their own concern; it affected everyone.

He dashed up the long ramp, desperate to find some-one else, someone able to decide. When he burst breath-less out of the airlock doors, Gaspard Desnoyer was just entering the voyant's apartment.

"Savant! You've got to come!" Dominique panted.

Gaspard stopped in surprise. "Dominique! Where is Aristide?"

"They're down in the control room. She's going to do something crazy."

Gaspard strode past him, grim-faced.

When they entered the control room again, Raspail and Aristide lay side by side in the same operator's chair, their heads together, temples touching. The wavering dis-continuity of a DI bubble engulfed their skulls. Through the heat-wave shimmer Dominique could see an absent, otherworldly expression on their faces.

They had escaped into Oracle. Into their private world where no one could follow.

"Did she say what she was doing?" Gaspard de-manded.

"Installing him on the machine."

"Damn!"

"Why?"

Gaspard quickly sat down at a keyboard. Symbols flit-ted across the screen. He stared at them intently. "She's disabled the controls, locked us out. I'll have to notify the other Instituts to quarantine Oracle till we can get another voyant in to stop her."

As he typed furiously, the screen went blank. He hit the desktop with his fists, swearing. "She's cut us off!"

"Why? What's going on?" Dominique said.

Gaspard turned to stare at Raspail's face as if seeing a new pattern. "Once that noetic structure gets loose in Oracle, it could corrupt the whole system. And if it gets transmitted to the other Instituts…" He clenched his fists. "Damn her! She *wants* an uncontrolled phase transition."

"What about Aristide?" Dominique asked. It seemed to be the question no one cared about.

"I hope he likes it in Oracle," Gaspard said grimly. "If she has her way, he's never going to make it out."

Gaspard crossed the room to the empty couch and bent over to check the DI mechanism on it. "She left it on! She knows there's no one here who can use it. Except…" He looked piercingly at Dominique.

"I've never been in Oracle," Dominique said, backing away.

"You've got the Bernaud pattern. You could survive."

"I wouldn't know where to start."

"Just find her. Contact her. See if she'll listen. It's the only thing we can do, Dominique."

Dominique's scalp hurt like fire where he had cut the chip away. This is my choice, he thought, staring at the empty couch. He didn't care about Sorel, or phase transitions. But to lock Aristide inside Oracle, never to escape…

Without stopping to think, he climbed onto the couch and lay back. "You operate it just like a normal helmet," Gaspard said. Dominique closed his eyes and breathed to evoke the alpha waves that triggered it.

🕯

At first he could make no sense at all of the jumble of colors: there was no clue to what was far, what near, or which portions connected to any others. Meaningless detail, everywhere. He spun around, bodiless, with the odd impression he was looking every direction at once. All the possible scenes were superimposed upon each other.

He spied a boundary amid the shifting mass of pixels, the first hint of structure he had seen. He tried to focus on it, to ignore everything else, so that it would resolve into a form. As he stared, other pieces of data began to accrete around it, to connect.

It was a glowing geometrical tree. And yet it was like an inside-out image; where he should have seen the surfaces of leaves, he saw openings—a tree of tiny caves in space. Focusing on one of the leaves, he saw that inside it were more caves, complex with stalactites that were themselves openings into other caves. A sense of infinite interiority barraged his mind; the whole world began oscillating between in and out. He struggled in panic against the torrent of input. All the information in the universe was hurtling toward him and away in the same motion; he was going to be crushed in an immense collision.

Darkness wrapped him. There was a calm force nearby, holding him, allowing him to see nothing. Far off in his body, he could feel his racing heart begin to slow.

"How did you get here?"

He did not exactly hear the words; they were almost pressed into his body. He recognized their source instinctively: Raspail. It was she who had intervened, given him the ability not to see.

Slowly, a form coalesced in front of him: Raspail in human shape, but younger, less worldworn than in life, as if she had not updated the symbol in many years.

"How did you get here?" she asked again.

"You told me to protect Aristide," Dominique said. "I'm doing it."

"You *are* a dog, aren't you?" she said. For some reason, it didn't strike Dominique as odd.

"What you just did was terribly dangerous," she said. "That was a five-dimensional phase space. If I hadn't been here the datastream could have thrown you into a feedback loop that would play in your mind forever."

She was rebuking him, but it was with such an intrigued tone that he couldn't feel shamed. It was as if he had done something very clever, and she didn't want him to know.

"I came to find you, and I did," he said.

"Your foolishness has delayed me," she said.

"I'm not going back without Aristide."

"You don't understand a thing. This is the habitat Aristide was created for. He is a symbiont that can explore its possibilities as we cannot do."

"I'll go away if he tells me to."

"You could not even perceive the space where he is now."

"Try me," he said.

She hesitated, and he sensed her curiosity, and something else—her desire for a witness. "The risk is yours," she said, then disappeared.

A data trail glowed like a fading line of fireflies, showing where she had gone. Taking a breath, like a diver going deep, Dominique followed.

He smashed through a boundary like a wall. Boisterous noise, color, texture screamed for his attention, spinning, dancing down overstimulated nerves. This time, he fought not to orient himself, not to understand, but merely to let pattern settle where it might.

Eventually, it did. He found himself in the pattern, yet able to view its totality at the same time. Here, distance and perspective did not blur detail into simplicity; faraway sights were as vivid as near ones, and he could view them from outside and inside simultaneously.

It was like a surreal landscape, if it was like anything. Above him rose a blue superlattice cliff, stepped back like shattered strata of rock. Beneath it was a glowing grove of branching symbols, crossing, tangling, complex as galaxies. He could see every detail of their structure, and the structure of their structure, regressing to infinity, dwarfing him with detail. For a moment he felt again the terror of not knowing his own scale.

"Careful," Raspail said, grasping his shoulder.

It brought him back, grounded him, to realize he *had* a shoulder, a boundary where he ended and the world began. He looked at Raspail, and she too had a shape, the gift of simplicity. He realized that, for all her harshness, she was not going to let him perish.

"This is the true fitness landscape of our species," Raspail said. "The Rinpoche and the Savants have seen only representations of it, simplified to caricature."

Everything was moving. Dominique watched vortexes of perturbation sweep across the land, and in their wake order melted into a twinkling, percolating sea. Islands rose; avalanches propagated in all directions, up as well as down.

"What am I seeing?" he asked.

"Data structures," Raspail said. "These are all visible algorithms, formulaic expressions. They have more variables than there are dimensions, so Oracle uses other sensory qualities to symbolize things."

The data structures did, in fact, excite more than one sense. In the valley ahead rose a forest of cool spearmint columns, smooth on his skin as glass; nearby a lemon-flavored prickle speared the air.

"What do the graphs mean?" he asked.

"The Savants seldom tell us," Raspail replied.

She turned around and looked across the land to where color and form ended. There, towering into the sky, was the gray wall of a massive thunderstorm. Within the turbulence, lightning flashed. Dominique drew back in fear, feeling as if threat were being transmitted directly into his brain without any intermediate evidence.

But as Raspail gazed at it, her representation bloomed into something intensely beautiful, shining with ardence. "That," she said, "is Aristide."

Dominique gazed at the storm. It dwarfed the landscape. "He's not human," he said.

"Not here," Raspail replied.

The storm stretched nearly from horizon to horizon ahead, blocking the way into the future. "Humanity will have to pass through him and become transformed," Raspail said. "Disequilibrium is the creative state. Without it, nothing will ever be new."

A bolt of lightning seared the land ahead. Dominique tried to imagine himself and all the people he knew passing through a boundary shaped by the strange chemistry of Aristide's mind, amplified by Oracle into an evolutionary force.

Raspail said, "All he needs to do now is withdraw from the body and become what you see forever."

She had lost her human shape and become a globe of filaments, a diatom graph. She floated upward, expanding till she was the size of all Sorel, and cast a webwork shadow over the valley; then she floated toward the storm-cloud. When she met it and was engulfed, she looked no larger than a pinprick.

Left alone, Dominique longed for the safety of his own body, waiting somewhere far away in the control room. He felt its pull, drawing him back, and for a moment the landscape before him turned two-dimensional and unreal. With an almost physical effort he pulled himself back. He could not run away now.

It only took a thought, and he was at the edge of the storm. It towered over him till he could see no sky. Wrapping his sense of himself tight, he plunged inside.

He was tumbling, battered, dropped by chaotic currents. Shreds of memory flew past, and a shivering rain drenched him. Too near, a thought ignited like a thunderbolt, jolting him back and leaving his fingers tingling. The roar was deafening.

A wind seized him and flung him forward, upside down, ripping at his limbs. He concentrated on his own identity.

There was silence. He found himself in a vast cylinder walled in by turbulent currents, like the eye of a hurricane. Ahead, against the dark glowed two symbols—diatom graphs. Raspail and Aristide. Somehow, he had reached the center of Aristide's mind, the place where structure resided.

The unfinished strands of Aristide's diatom graph were twinkling. Raspail reached out, strangely gentle, to break one off; but Aristide's graph pulled back like a live thing fearing pain.

"Please, Aristide," Raspail said. "I have to make you safe from desecration."

The globe drifted back within her reach. Dominique watched, feeling there was something he ought to do, but not knowing what. Within the storm wall he could hear a tiny voice, wailing.

She reached out quickly then and snapped a twig of Aristide's mind. For a moment the diatom graph hung motionless. Then, with a brittle popping sound, overstrained branches began to break. Raspail cried out as she saw the structure begin to collapse. Before she could act, the walls of the storm burst in on them.

In a moment of pure instinct, Dominique made a flying leap and caught the crumbling sphere of Aristide's mind like a football, circling it with his body, trying to hold its shaky partitions together. A gust of storm bludgeoned him from one side, sending him spinning. He glimpsed Raspail's graph, caught in the storm's power.

Then he centered on his own solidity, trying to track his way back to a place where he was real.

His hands were gripping the edge of the couch, tendons white. The control room was far away down a dark tunnel. He struggled toward it. Nothing felt right. The air grated like sandpaper on his cheek. The light kept dissolving like salt in water. He eyes couldn't focus together, and he saw weird double images, one close, one far.

Gradually, the broken pieces of the world came to rest in a new order, precariously balanced. A face was looking down on him. His name echoed strangely in the vault behind his eyes.

"Dominique! It's Savant Barrère. You're all right now. You're safe."

"Safe?" Dominique repeated. His thinking felt slow and viscous. He tried to sit up. "Is Aristide all right?"

The savant didn't answer. Dominique realized there were others in the room, clustered around the operator's chair behind him. Gaspard was there. For a moment his eyes met Dominique's. He looked wasted and old.

Dominique swung his legs over the edge of the couch to stand up. "Stiff knees!" Barrère said in his ear, and it was a good thing, because his legs would have collapsed under his weight. He pushed forward.

Aristide's eyes were open and staring at the ceiling, but there was nothing behind them—no thought, no pain, no pleasure. All the lightning quickness, all the madcap energy was gone. "You saved his life," Barrère said softly. It made Dominique want to laugh bitterly. To what purpose? He might as well have saved a heap of broken glass.

Raspail lay curled in fetal position. He could not see her face, but her posture looked unnatural. He saw Gaspard holding her hand, and it was from the savant's face that he knew she had not made it back.

"Dominique, what you did was a miracle," Barrère said at his side. "No one could have done better. When you are trained, you will be the greatest voyant who ever lived."

He looked at her then, wondering what drove these people. In a voice that sounded like broken glass being ground underfoot he said, "To hell with Oracle. To hell with Sorel. To hell with all of you."

In the silence, he could hear little voices in his mind, repeating his words.

High atop the tallest pinnacle in Sorel, the Rinpoche's Voice and Gaspard Desnoyer stood with headnets on, staring at an empty spot in the air three feet in front of them.

If she closed her eyes, Naidu could practically feel the turbulent rush of time around her, tugging chaotically, as if Sorel were a pebble in the rapids. The discontinuity was upon them now.

At her side, Gaspard frowned nervously at the blank air. "They are definitely not the same," he said. "Something happened."

"That is scarcely surprising," Naidu answered.

The headnets showed them both the same display. The basic structure of the two diatom graphs was the same—a perfect Bernaud diagram. But the second was far more complex, as if it had grown new branches overnight.

"When was it taken?" Gaspard asked.

"Just as he was leaving Oracle. The machine monitors the voyants' graphs entering and leaving, but Raspail had disabled all the safety devices."

At a command from Gaspard, the headnets subtracted the first pattern from the second, showing only the changes. They were thin and ghostly, filaments like spiderweb.

"You know what it looks like?" Gaspard said.

"I know what I *think* it looks like. What do you see?"

With a flick of his eyes Gaspard brought up another graph, one they had all seen for the first time only a day before. Its asymmetry was as unsettling now as then.

Gaspard said, "It's as if parts of Aristide's graph have become superimposed on Dominique's, or grafted to it."

Naidu nodded. "It is not impossible. After all, we are dealing with a being designed to inhabit another system."

"So instead of being installed in Oracle, he became installed in Dominique?"

"An attenuated version. You notice it isn't as complex as the original."

Gaspard pulled off his headnet and balled it up in his fist. "So Raspail's legacy continues. I don't know how we're going to fix this."

Inside her, Naidu could feel the sad, ancient presence of a man who no longer existed in his own body. Not until now had she seen empirical evidence of what instinct had long told her, that it was possible to become blended with another being: To carry forward a legacy of another's thought, not just in metaphor, but in measurable fact.

"Why do you feel we need to fix it?" she said.

Gaspard looked shocked. "We owe it to Dominique," he said. "It's the only moral thing, to restore him." He paused. "Besides, we can't let him come in contact with Oracle till this is solved. Even this version of Aristide's graph could contaminate the system."

"Ah," Naidu said. It was an eloquent syllable, expressing understanding, skepticism, and gentle humor at the same time. She had said it inadvertently in the Rinpoche's voice. Before, she would have thought nothing of the mimicry: mere force of habit. Now, it surprised her.

Gaspard was too preoccupied to notice. "Yes, I know," he said. "Dominique says he doesn't want to stay. He'll change his mind. He has to. He was born to be a voyant."

"We could, of course, make him want it," Naidu said quietly. "Raspail proved that. But it doesn't mean we should."

"I'm not proposing that," Gaspard said.

"You are proposing to change his mind."

"To *persuade* him. We can't let Raspail's crimes prevent us from that. This is Dominique's duty, his destiny. And we are desperate. Without a voyant, we are navigating blind."

"It all depends on the scale on which you see things." Naidu's gaze drifted to the window, where the sheer face of Mont Chatoyer stood against the stars. "The question is, on which scale does the right path lie? The scale of history, or the scale of human lives?"

"The Rinpoche would tell us to act for the benefit of Sorel."

"I know what the Rinpoche would say." Naidu spoke with the authority of utter conviction. It was a new voice for her—her own.

Gaspard was searching her face, trying to divine who was speaking. She smiled at him, for the first time utterly certain of who she was. It was like clasping hands with an old friend. "Perhaps some day our algorithms will be able to map the landscape of ethics, or plot the trajectories of love," she said.

It was a paradox, that it should take another being to make her more herself. Perhaps love was a species of phase transition. She smiled regretfully. "But we are not there yet."

☦

Dominique came down the mountain with his pack on his back. The road was solid under his feet. The air was cool, and even the water seeping into his boots felt good. Real life was made of ordinary textures like this. He had never appreciated them before.

The unreal, detached feeling that had stayed after his adventure into Oracle was wearing off on its own, just as he had told Gaspard it would. He was glad to feel like himself again, without any of Sorel's so-called help.

The bus was coming down the street, toward its stop at the hotel. He ran to meet it. No one gave him a second glance as he bought a ticket home with the cash Gaspard had loaned him.

"Call me when you get there," the savant had said, "so I know you made it."

He had looked so anxious that Dominique had said, "Don't worry, it's not hard to take a bus." Only a person with a dozen degrees would think so, he didn't add.

For a moment he'd thought there was something Gaspard wanted to tell him; but in the end the savant only said, "Your common sense is your biggest asset, Dominique. Listen to it."

"You sound like a fortune cookie," slipped out of Dominique's mouth before he could stop it. At first Gaspard looked startled at the uncharacteristic impudence, but then he smiled. The expression looked so remorseful that Dominique's heart went out to him.

The bus doors sighed shut. Dominique watched out the window as they passed the bookstore on the way out of town. He felt a sad satisfaction that Gabriel was going to be free to be Gabriel, to mess up his life if that was what he wanted, without any interference from Sorel. For a moment he could see the possibilities before his brother, branching like an infinitely complex decision tree. His own future was woven into it, a filigree of choices. The landscape outside became unreal and far away; only the pattern existed. With an effort, Dominique concentrated on who he was and where he ended.

The window had become fogged with his breath. He wiped it with his sleeve. The world, with all its mud and sunlight, was still out there, beyond the glass. All he had to do was remember that, and everything would be all right.

About the Author

Carolyn Ives Gilman has been publishing science fiction and fantasy for almost twenty years. Her first novel, *Halfway Human,* published by Avon/Eos in 1998, was called "one of the most compelling explorations of gender and power in recent SF" by *Locus* magazine. Her short fiction has appeared in magazines and anthologies such as *Fantasy and Science Fiction, Bending the Landscape, The Year's Best Science Fiction, Realms of Fantasy, The Best From Fantasy & Science Fiction, Interzone, Universe, Full Spectrum,* and others. Her fiction has been translated into Italian, Russian, and German. In 1992 she was a finalist for the Nebula Award for her novella, "The Honeycrafters."

In her professional career, Gilman is a historian specializing in 18th- and early 19th-century North American history, particularly frontier and Native history. Her most recent nonfiction book, *Lewis and Clark: Across the Divide,* was published in 2003 by Smithsonian Books. She has been a guest lecturer at the Library of Congress, Harvard University, and Monticello, and has been interviewed on *All Things Considered* (NPR), *Talk of the Nation* (NPR), *History Detectives* (PBS), and the History Channel.

Carolyn Ives Gilman lives in St. Louis and works for the Missouri Historical Society as a historian and museum curator.